Never Goodbye

The Barrington Billionaires

Book Seven

Ruth Cardello

Author Contact
website: RuthCardello.com
email: ruthcardello@gmail.com
Facebook: Author Ruth Cardello
Twitter: RuthieCardello
Goodreads
goodreads.com/author/show/4820876.Ruth_Cardello
Bookbub
bookbub.com/authors/ruth-cardello

New York Times and *USA Today* bestselling author Ruth Cardello returns with a hilarious addition to the Barrington Billionaire series.

In the Barrington family, Ian is the fixer. He lives a double life—one that has provided him with the skills to save his family more than once. Reuniting with the brother they'd all believed was dead has shaken him to the core. He is driven to find the responsible party regardless of the consequences.

Claire Wendell's best friend recently married into the very powerful, very troubled Barrington family. When she stepped away from her own life to help Annie and Kade settle into theirs, she had no idea it would put her on a possible suspect list.

She's bold enough to stand up to Ian and intuitive enough to see past his anger, but love may not be enough to protect the family when the truth about the woman who raised Kade is revealed.

How important is the truth?

Is it worth losing everything?

Copyright

Print Edition

ISBN: 978-1-7324201-5-1

An original work of Ruth Cardello, 2018.

Dedication

To my brother Gerry. Thank you for always being there for me.

Chapter One

Boston, Massachusetts
Kade and Annie's Wedding Reception, Present Day

SORRY GRANT, THERE is no way in hell either of your wife's brothers will survive what I will do to them as soon I get my hands free. Ian Barrington was in pain, but it wasn't from the duct tape that bound both his wrists and ankles. Nor from the strip across his mouth. He wasn't suffering from a concussion nor was his body bruised from the pummeling one would expect to accompany a kidnapping. Even the physical discomfort from being slung over the shoulder of one of the Neanderthals who'd carried him into the hotel's staircase wasn't what bothered him the most.

No, what was slowly killing him was how the two men had completely taken him by surprise. Closer to seven feet than six, Connor and Dylan were born to wear plaid, not twins but so similar in appearance most assumed they were and dumb enough that they should have been harmless.

Idiots could be confident little fuckers.

What do they want?

Ransom? They already know they'll never be homeless, and

with our support their father's business is booming.

But for some, no amount of assistance is enough. They want it all.

Or did someone hire them to take me out? And if so—who?

Ian wasn't naïve to how far his enemies would go for revenge. Unfortunately, he'd crossed enough people in his life that the list of who would want him gone was too extensive to be useful.

How deep was his family compromised? He didn't want to imagine Viviana, his brother's wife, could be involved. Grant had never looked happier and the two had a child together.

This was more likely a crime born from opportunity and temptation. These two might have been approached by someone connected to the Columbian drug baron Ian had helped the Mexican government crack down on. The one who was currently being extradited to New York for the crimes he'd committed there as well.

Loyalty could be bought.

No, if Rojas wanted me dead, he would have used his own men.

The same was true for any one of the dictators Ian had helped the US government topple or the foreign companies he'd negotiated against, if they were wise to his involvement, which he'd been careful to ensure they wouldn't be.

Even his CIA connections knew only what he wanted them to. His official title was International Political Consultant, but his relationship with the government was much more complicated than it looked in their database. He brought them information. When he agreed with the cause, he used his connections to sway the outcome of an event. Sometimes, when no one else could, he resolved a situation himself.

A much younger Ian had followed his father's footsteps and gone into politics, only to discover that very little was actually decided by the elected officials. Presidents came and went. The house and the senate debated, but little was accomplished. When he realized that so much in the news was a circus meant to entertain and distract, he sought out the company of those truly shaping the global landscape.

He watched.

Learned.

Made sure many of them owed him a favor.

All the while, his own wealth and influence had grown until he'd earned his own seat at the table. Most of his peers were less hands-on. They met under the strict Chatham House Rule: exchange information and formulate plans, with the understanding that nothing that was said would ever be attributed to any of the participants. It all sounded nefarious, but more often than not it was a bunch of old, rich men grasping for ways to retain their piece of the pie. There were some however, like Ian, who'd come for the power rather than the wealth.

The CIA considered him dangerous but necessary.

Somewhere between a traitor and a hero.

He didn't like the term vigilante. Simply put, his allegiance had always been first to humanity then to his country. So yes, when it was in the best interest of the innocent, he could orchestrate the fall of a world leader or get a political prisoner released.

And when it wasn't . . . he could be intentionally ineffective.

He'd built a network of influence that knew no boundaries, but he used it only for what his conscience allowed. In his youth he'd been a helpless witness to his mother's suffering. His one goal had been to never feel that way again.

By his early thirties, he'd surpassed even what he'd imagined possible. Although his name would never be in history books, the improved living conditions of the areas of the world he'd championed was gratification enough. Clean water, adequate housing, and access to medicine were basic human needs that far too many didn't have. Wars were fought over oil and resources for the rich. He battled in the shadows, doing what he could to ensure those in power did more good than harm.

He'd been riding high, feeling damn near invincible . . . until Grant had found the brother his family had been told had died at childbirth.

Although Ian had been in grade school when they'd lost Kade, he cursed himself for never circling back to ask questions. Had he done any research at all, he would have discovered that the doctors and nurses involved in delivering Kade had all died soon afterward. One from a fatal car accident, one from suicide, two drowned. The truth was right there—so painfully obvious it sickened Ian that he'd missed it.

He easily could have hunted down Pamela, the woman

who'd run to Australia with his stolen brother and raised him as her own. He could have brought Kade home so much sooner. Even though he'd been young, he remembered his mother crying and vehemently saying again and again that she'd held Kade . . . that he was alive.

No one had believed her. In retrospect, her subsequent mental breakdown made sense. She was right. She knew, but that hadn't been enough, even for those who loved her.

His family had spent the next thirty years mourning the death of a child who wasn't dead and walking on eggshells around their mother, thinking her unstable when she was truly the strongest of them all. So much unnecessary pain that thus far no one had been held accountable for.

So, yes, finding out what really happened back then had become an obsession of Ian's. *Is that why I'm duct-taped? Am I getting too close to the truth for someone's comfort?*

The door to the hallway slammed shut behind Dylan. "That's the biggest laundry cart you could find?" He shifted to adjust the weight of Ian.

"He'll fit," Connor said with confidence. "Well, if we fold him up."

Oh, hell no. Ian threw his weight to one side, hoping to send Dylan off-balance, but he was remarkably sure-footed.

"Easy, Ian," Dylan growled. "We just need a minute to figure this out. What do you mean fold him up? He's not going to work with us."

"Maybe you were right—we should have drugged him."

"You think?"

"Don't get all pissy. That's not helping. We could knock

him out, but I read that can give people brain damage."

"What if we cut off some of his oxygen just long enough for him to pass out? Does that do anything bad?"

What the fuck?

"I'm not a doctor, but it sounds like it would. No, try putting him in head first."

Ian shook his head back and forth. Dylan said, "He doesn't like that idea. I wouldn't either. Probably painful."

"Okay," Connor scratched his chin. "Put him in feet first and see what happens."

As soon as his bound feet hit the solid bottom of the laundry cart, Ian found his balance. He stood straight up and glared at the two meatheads who were studying the situation like children confused about why a square block won't fit through a circular hole.

"Sit," Connor commanded.

Ian didn't budge.

"He's not a dog," Dylan snapped.

"Do you have a better idea?"

Ian was not shocked when Dylan didn't.

Am I already dead? Is this hell? Because it feels like hell.

Hands on his hips, Dylan asked, "Hey, Einstein, even if we get him in there, how are we going to carry him up twenty floors in the cart?"

"Shit, I didn't think about that."

Twenty floors? Where are they taking me?

Ian began to slowly, subtly twist his wrists back and forth. He'd fisted his hands when they'd bound them, so there was a little give to the tape, but for idiots they'd done a surprisingly effective job with the restraints. Not only had they gone around, but they'd circled between, which made it more difficult, although not impossible to break free.

"You get him, I'll carry the cart. We'll figure out how to stuff him in when we get to Claire's floor."

Claire? Maid of honor and the best friend of his new sister-in-law, Annie.

The beautiful brunette who'd been circling around his family the last few months.

Circling around his dreams at night as well.

The same woman he'd caught listening in to a recent conversation he'd had with his brother Asher. He'd told Asher he didn't trust her—said as much to her face afterward. Still, what would her motive be?

Money?

Revenge? They say hell knows no fury like a woman scorned, but this is a bit much.

Pausing for a breath after ten floors, Connor said, "Hey, Dylan. Text Claire. Tell her to meet us at her room."

"Done. I can't believe this was so easy. I mean, didn't you think Ian would put up more of a fight?"

Ian groaned. Yeah, that still stung.

"He would have if we'd used chloroform like you wanted to. Good thing I looked it up on my phone. It's not like in the movies. That shit takes five minutes to work. Plus, sometimes it's lethal."

"I was joking about using it. Where would we have even gotten some? Do you think I fucking walk around with shit like that in my pocket?"

"You sounded serious."

"You're an idiot."

"And you're weak if you thought Ian's heavy. I could carry him up forty floors without breaking a sweat."

"I didn't say he was heavy. I just don't like to carry men around."

"You think I do?"

"I don't know what you like, and I don't judge."

"You're going to eat my fist in a minute."

"Bring it."

"I will if you don't shut up." Connor spun on the step, knocking Ian's head against the wall as he did. Ian swore beneath the tape.

"Hey, don't kill him," Dylan said. "I actually like him. I mean, it's annoying how he thinks he's better than us, but it's not his fault he was born with a silver stick up his ass."

Connor started walking up the stairs again. "A spoon."

"No one puts a spoon up their ass."

"I don't think anyone puts a stick there either. It's a saying: silver spoon or stick up your ass. Not silver stick."

"Don't pretend you know the difference. A few etiquette lessons from Claire doesn't make you an expert on everything."

"Whatever. You're not going to put me in a bad mood, Dylan. I feel like Robin Hood."

"What?"

"Taking from the rich and giving to the poor."

"That doesn't even fit what we're doing."

"Yeah, in my head it made more sense. What I'm saying

is I feel good about this." Connor stopped and lowered Ian to his feet, leaning him back against the wall. "I have an idea."

Dylan placed the cart beside Ian. "Okay, shoot."

No, don't shoot.

"Is there a bag in the bottom of the cart? We could put it over his head and just carry him to her room like that. Forget the cart."

With the duct tape almost loose enough to free his hands, Ian bent into a seated position.

"Just a towel, but I think he wants to sit in the cart," Dylan said.

Connor sighed, picked Ian up, and placed him inside the cart. Ian sat down, his head showing above the top, and used the position to completely free his hands. He kept them tucked behind him, though. This time he was the one who would have the element of surprise on his side. Connor placed the towel over his head and one of them opened the door to the hallway. Completely concealed as he was wheeled, Ian undid the tape from around his ankles.

He was about to remove the tape from his mouth when a knock on a door was followed by the cart moving forward abruptly enough to send him off-balance.

He was still trying to right himself when he heard Connor say, "Claire, we have a present for you . . ."

Chapter Two

Kade and Annie's Wedding Reception, two hours earlier

WEDDINGS WERE SUPPOSED to be a time of celebration. They were all about sharing the joy of a loving couple.

Claire Wendell slipped out of the main reception area into a quiet hallway. *I am happy for Annie and Kade, I just need a little fresh air.*

The hallway led to a small garden courtyard. Claire pushed a glass door open and breathed in the mix of flowers and night air. Most people probably used the area to smoke, however Claire didn't have that vice.

Annie teased her about being regimented, but Claire's childhood had been full of uncertainty and chaos. Nothing and no one would ever take her back to that place. Structure made her feel safe. Routine brought her calm. Neither her success with her business nor her dress size had come to her easily. She'd fought for both.

No sugar. No alcohol. Nothing that could be described as unhealthy or unproductive. She'd built her business, Claire's Accountability Coaching Agency, on the idea of confidence via control, and she lived that mantra. Life was full of the unexpected. It often wasn't fair, and it showed no mercy to the weak, but if a person kept their life structured and free of distraction, they could survive the worst of it.

She was a living example to her clients, many of whom had catapulted to success before reaching out to her, yet were plagued by doubt. Everything changed when people came into money or fame. Relationships changed . . . even solid ones were tested. There was a reason so many people fell apart when they made it to the top . . . you can't take everyone with you, and it's a whole different world up there.

A person either adapted or imploded.

People thought they wanted fame until every move they made was dissected—and fed to the masses often harshly and inaccurately. Demon or saint, the media chose how to portray someone, and many people fell into the trap of defining themselves in terms of how the public saw them.

Claire taught them how to focus their energy inward toward proactive, achievable goals and to define themselves in their own terms.

Focus on what is within your control to affect and not on the noise of what you cannot.

The calm she'd cultivated for herself and marketed to others, however, was being challenged by a growing fear that stepping away from her business might have damaged it more than she'd imagined it could.

Almost daily, she received another email from a client who had, in her absence, come to the conclusion they didn't require her services. None of her assurances that her time away was coming to an end swayed them. Apparently stepping away had given them time to see she'd organized their lives enough that they were self-sufficient. A few had found alternative support and didn't want the disruption of switching back.

They say no good deed goes unpunished . . . and that pride goes before a fall.

They're right.

Almost two months away, what did I think would happen? Did I honestly believe I could simply return and everything would pick up exactly how I'd left it?

Claire's clients had been supportive at first. Annie and Kade's story was all over the media. He was the Australian boy next door who'd discovered he was also the child of one of the richest families in the US. Annie was the hard-working woman who had loved him poor and was now living out her own Cinderella story. That was the ideal, romanticized version of their journey.

The reality was Annie had a business she didn't want to walk away from, and Kade had needed to learn how to navigate the constant scrutiny of being an overnight celebrity.

When Annie had asked Claire to help them with that transition, she'd agreed without hesitation. That was what she did. So, she'd helped redesign the vision of Annie's transport company. She'd introduced Kade to the methods her other clients utilized when dealing with the public. He'd needed to learn how to be himself while not giving the media anything that could be used against his family—his US one or his Australian one.

They'd become Claire's only clients, while not technically being clients at all.

All of which is my fault. I could have said no at any time. I could have stepped back, addressed the concerns of my own business, and circled back to help them in a way that wouldn't have cost me my clientele.

My misstep was overconfidence.

I don't regret saying yes.

Which part would I have refused?

When Annie and Kade were still reeling from meeting the rest of the family he'd only recently realized he had and they'd asked me to meet them as well?

When they asked me to stay and do what I do best—build a plan for success?

How about when, out of gratitude to Annie and Kade, Clay Landon had decided to make their wedding into the most extravagant event Boston had ever seen? Someone needed to remind him that acrobats were not necessary during the cocktail hour.

Should I have said no to helping Viviana's brothers, Dylan and Connor, prepare for the wedding?

Maybe.

Every door had been open to me in Melbourne. What if they don't reopen? It was humbling to see how quickly her financial situation had changed. Like rats fleeing a sinking ship, news of one high profile person no longer using Claire's service had the rest in a near stampede to leave her as well.

Confidence was difficult to maintain in the face of that.

I could have told Annie that my business was suffering and asked her for compensation for my time here. Her new husband is a billionaire, and they were essentially my clients.

But I didn't want to ask a friend for money.

Pride.

Claire paced the small garden and assured herself she could fix everything that was falling apart. Annie was married now. She was heading off on her honeymoon the next day. *I'm free to go home and put my business back together.*

Even the extra ten pounds I put on . . . it'll come back off.

Every decision I make is a step toward or away from chaos. Annie is like a sister to me, and I don't regret helping her, but it is time for me to return to my life.

She hiked up the hem of her gown and sat on a bench that blissfully was temporarily hidden by an enormous planter. One deep breath in. One slowly released breath out. Breathe in. Breathe out. *All I need to do is break this down into achievable tasks. Once I get home, I'll reach out to my clients again. What I do is important. They'll see that. If they don't, I'll build a new base of clientele. I've done it before. I can do it again.*

The door of the garden opened. Claire would have announced herself, but didn't when she recognized the voice of Annie's now brother-in-law, Asher Barrington, and he sounded irritated. "Ian, we're at a wedding, not a funeral. Mom asked me to find out what's bothering you, that's the only reason I'm doing this." Before Ian responded, Asher continued, "If you're still obsessing about Pamela you need to get over it. It's ancient history."

"Accepting stories at face value has proven to be a destructive pattern for our family," Ian, the only single Barrington son, said in a cold tone. "One I no longer support."

"We found Kade. He's happy. Mom and Dad are happy. They actually like Pam and Dave. Your ongoing investigation into Kade's kidnapping was understandable at first. Now it's just annoying. No one cares."

"They should. They should absolutely care whether Pamela is an innocent who hid a child to protect him or is a criminal who escaped and is using him to protect herself now."

"Kade is no longer a child, and even if you found out that the woman who raised him as her own was a horrible human being before she ran off to Australia with him . . . who gives a fuck? He wasn't hurt by the experience. In fact, it's insulting how much happier he is than the rest of us. Sometimes you have to leave well enough alone."

"That's precisely the philosophy that kept us from finding him."

Asher let out an audible sigh. "Listen, I get the guilt thing. Do you think I don't wish I'd believed Mom when she said Kade was alive? Sure. Nothing I can do about that now, though. I can imagine with all of your government connections you'd feel even worse. I mean, if any of us were going to find him, it should have been you. That Grant was the one—"

"Is this you trying to make me feel better?"

"No, this is me waking you the fuck up. Let it go, Ian."

"I can't, Asher. I need to know what happened." Ian's voice was guttural and tormented.

Not wanting to miss a word, Claire leaned forward in her chair, causing it to scrape against the stone floor.

And froze.

Shit.

Had they heard her?

She waited.

"You need to focus on something else. What about Annie's friend, Claire? She's not ugly."

Claire sat up. Not ugly? This was why eavesdropping was a bad idea. Only in movies did people overhear something good.

"I have zero interest in her," Ian countered.

Ouch.

Well, the feeling is mutual, buddy.

Sure, Ian had the classic good looks of the Barrington clan, and she might originally have found that distracting, but he had the personality of a shoe smeared with shit. He was that much of a downer.

"That's a shame, because there's a plot afoot to nudge the two of you together. Emily asked me what I thought. Oh, shit, I wasn't supposed to say anything to you. Try to look surprised when it happens."

"I'm not the type who appreciates surprises, but don't worry, I would have quickly seen through any attempts to hook us up. Very little that people think is hidden actually is."

Claire covered her mouth with one hand and told herself

he wasn't referring to her being in the garden with them. She was well concealed.

"Whatever, just don't let on that I said anything. All the women like Claire, and I don't want to be the reason she doesn't marry into this family."

"Don't worry. You wouldn't be the reason. She's the polar opposite of everything I find attractive. Who wants a woman whose profession is literally to tell people what to do? I could tolerate that for about thirty seconds."

What an asshole.

"Fair enough."

"I don't trust her, either. On one hand, she's supposedly a moderately successful businesswoman, but how fast did she drop everything when she had the chance to come to Boston and have her name associated with ours?"

Claire nearly surged to her feet in protest but stopped herself just in time. She shouldn't be surprised by his low opinion of her, he looked at everyone through that same dark lens.

Asher interjected, "Okay, so you don't like her either. I'd ask you who else is on your shit list, but I honestly don't care. Do us all a favor—just smile and keep your issues to yourself."

"Good talk, Asher," Ian said with sarcasm.

The door of the garden opened. "You coming back to the reception?"

"In a minute."

"Hey, I didn't mean it when I said I don't care." In a lighter tone, Asher added, "If you need to talk, I'm always here. We'll figure it out. I don't want my kid to have crazy uncles."

Ian said in dry tone, "I'm all set."

A moment after the door to the garden closed, Claire stood and found her escape route blocked by Ian, arms folded across his chest, with the same closed off expression she'd come to associate with him. "Enjoying yourself?"

DID SHE REALLY think I wouldn't know she was there?

Claire looked deliciously flustered, a fact that annoyed Ian. He'd meant what he said about her not being his type. He preferred women with a little more meat on them, softer both in curves and personality. His cock, though, had formed its own opinion of her. As his blood rushed south, he reminded himself that his dick hadn't had a deciding vote since high school. "I was here before you and your brother arrived. For your information, there's nothing I find appealing about you, either. So your opinion of me and my business matters . . . let's see . . . oh, not at all."

He told himself to walk away.

Her eyes widened when he took a step closer. Hell, he was just as shocked by the move. "Is that so?"

"Yes," she said in a tight, low voice.

He stepped closer still. She stood her ground, her small breasts heaving beneath the bodice of her gown. He didn't want to imagine cupping them, kissing his way from one to another, but once he did he couldn't think of much else. "So, you don't find me attractive?" He leaned down so his face was just above hers.

It was an electric moment, the kind that froze time.

Her breath warmed his lips. "I can tolerate you for about thirty seconds."

A smile pulled at the corner of his mouth. "I knew you were listening."

"Which makes you even more of an asshole."

"I'm not sorry. Your silence proved my point."

Her shoulders squared. "I didn't want to intrude."

"You're beyond that."

"What does that mean?"

"It means I don't like how you've practically moved in with my parents, and I don't believe Annie's the only reason you're here."

"Why else would I be?" She studied his face for a minute then shook her head and took a step back. "Wow. You know what? Keep your paranoid accusations to yourself. You don't need to put another thought into me or my motives. I fly home tomorrow."

A lifetime of being told to do just that had Ian's temper flaring. He stepped closer and growled. "You'd better be exactly what you claim to be."

Eye blazing with anger, she asked, "Are you threatening me, Ian?"

"If I am . . . are you scared? You shouldn't be unless you're hiding something."

She looked down at her watch. "Looks like our thirty seconds are over." With that, she spun on her heel and strode out of the garden. "I'm heading back to the reception. Stay away from me, Ian."

Ian folded his arms back over his chest and told himself he didn't care if he'd upset her. Hating him was safer for her than giving into the desire he'd glimpsed in her eyes. Okay, so maybe he'd lied about her not being his taste. She'd have been in his bed a long time ago if they'd met in any other way, if she wasn't the best friend of Kade's wife . . . if her accent didn't constantly remind him of a chapter of the Barrington history that never should have been . . .

After his mother's breakdown, the focus of the family had been keeping things calm for her. No one cried. No one yelled. And problems? They'd dealt with them on their own.

It had made Asher into "a hammer."

Grant into a control freak when it came to money.

Driven Andrew to the edge.

Made Lance so soft Ian struggled to connect with him.

And Kenzi . . . she'd suffered in silence until finding her voice.

Someone needs to pay for all that, and I will find that person.

Run away, Claire.

The best I could give you is an angry fuck—and I don't need one more thing to regret.

Chapter Three

SHAKING AND BLINKING back angry tears, Claire burst out of the garden and rushed blindly in the opposite direction from the reception. She stopped and rested against the wall of the first hallway.

I should have walked out as soon as they entered the garden.

I should have announced my presence.

Her hand came up to her lips. *He didn't have to be cruel, though.*

Ian's general state of unhappiness had been the topic of more than one discussion with Annie, whose major concern was Kade and what it would do to him if Ian found anything damning about the woman who had raised him.

"Do you think he might?" Claire had asked.

"I don't know," Annie had said. "A few months ago, if you'd told me Kade wasn't biologically Pamela's I wouldn't have believed it. I understand why Ian wants to know what happened back then, but I pray he doesn't find what he's looking for."

"What is that?"

"Someone to punish. At first, I thought Kade had it

rough because his life was pulled out from beneath his feet. Suddenly he didn't know who he was. But, he's working his way through that."

"With your help."

"I'm only able to be his rock because you've been mine," Annie had kindly said. "Ian blames himself for so many things he couldn't have known. He was too young. Grant says Ian has always been the fixer in the family. Even Asher turns to him for help, and he's never let them down. He can't fix this, and he's not handling that well."

"Even if he found someone who was responsible—it wouldn't change what happened."

"We know. I don't think that Ian sees opening up that part of the past has more potential of hurting his family than healing them."

People who are hurt often don't realize when they're hurting others.

I tell my clients that all the time.

It's our choice, though, how much we let their unhappiness affect us.

She raised a hand to her lips. There had been a moment in the garden when she'd thought he might kiss her. *And I wanted him to.*

That was the hardest admission to make to herself.

He's a miserable man.

A dangerous one.

I don't need that in my life.

How can I be attracted to him?

She groaned. *Maybe it's those dark, brooding eyes.*

Those arms that look like they could easily carry me.

And part of me wants to be the one who shows him . . .

She smacked herself in the forehead.

Oh, my God. I think I can change him.

Habits change.

Character doesn't.

I should thank him for being such an asshole. That's all that has stopped me from making a huge mistake.

She opened her eyes and clapped her hands together. She needed to stop wasting time thinking about Ian and focus on what mattered—getting home tomorrow and getting her clients back. One more day in Boston, then her life would go back to normal.

"On my worst day, in a tux or naked, I am better looking than you," a man boomed, and Claire straightened off the wall at the sound of Connor's voice. Since Annie had married into the Barrington clan, her sister-in-law's brothers were sort of family.

Sort of.

Three. Two . . .

"Stop picturing me naked," Dylan taunted then made a pained sound in response when Connor socked him in the shoulder as they rounded the corner.

"I didn't. You're disgusting," Connor protested. "It's a saying."

"No it's not. No one says that." Dylan nodded to Claire. "Claire, tell Connor I'm right—as usual."

"I've never heard the expression, but I'm Australian, so it could be a thing." She forced a smile. Viviana said they were rough around the edges because they'd lost their mother at a young age. Claire could see that, but they were also suffering a bit from Peter Pan syndrome. One day, maybe, they'd want to grow up—but even though they were in their late twenties, that day hadn't come yet.

And probably wouldn't any time soon. God had blessed the two of them with strong, square jaws, thick blond hair, and shoulders that belonged on linebackers. Women flocked to them. Men couldn't intimidate them. What motivation did either of them have to change?

Their most appealing characteristic? Their devotion to their sister. They were only in tuxes because they knew it was important to Viviana.

Claire had to admit she'd grown fond of them. They'd gone shopping together, practiced which utensils to use for what course during fancy meals, and that bread should never be thrown across a table. They bickered, but their loyalty to each other was evident. It made her wish she had siblings. What was life like when there was someone to share the load?

Connor whined, "I need a drink."

"You both promised you wouldn't at the wedding," Claire reminded him gently.

"Annie's parents own a beer brewery. We'd be supporting their business by tossing a few back," Dylan added in frustrated tone. "I asked Kade, and he said he didn't care."

Claire gave his shoulder a supportive pat. Part of her hoped they wouldn't change. In a world full of people who obsessed about what other people thought about them, these two were blissfully either unaware or indifferent. Many of her clients could benefit from that kind of confidence. "What are you two doing out here?"

"We're so bored." Dylan looked around the hall as if concerned he'd been overheard. "It was a nice wedding. When do we get to leave?"

Connor shook his head. "That's rude. It'll be over when the fat lady sings."

Dylan shook his head. "*What* lady?"

With a smirk, Connor said, "He doesn't get proverbs."

I'm not sure you do, either.

With a shrug, Dylan said, "And I don't like the word fat. I think a little extra weight on a woman is sexy. The skinny ones are too fragile." He looked Claire over. "No offense."

"None taken." She ran a hand over her eyes. *My ego is taking a beating today.*

"And I'd want a woman who could sing, that would be nice for when we're in the woods and the radio doesn't get reception," Dylan continued, looking down the hall as if such a woman were about to materialize.

"There is no fat lady." Connor sighed.

Claire meant to laugh, but it came out sounding like a sob. The brothers exchanged a panicked look. Connor said, "Now look what you did. She's upset."

"Oh, man," Dylan ran his hand through his hair. "Claire, we're just joking around. I'm sure plenty of men think you're hot."

"I'm not upset with *you*." Her voice cracked during her denial.

It's me.

I need to get home.

"I'm sorry. It's been an emotional day."

The door to the garden opened. Ian frowned in their direction then walked off toward the reception. Connor looked from Claire to Ian and back. "Did he say something to you?"

Claire took a calming breath, but the truth spilled out of her. "Nothing I should have been surprised by. He was just—Ian."

Dylan grunted. "Don't let him get to you. He doesn't like us either."

"You don't know that . . ." Claire started to say, then stopped. It was true. Grant called Connor and Dylan meatheads, but there was affection in his tone when he did. Ian wasn't as kind. "He can't like anyone until he likes himself. I'd explain that to him, but I'd have to tie him up, practically gag him, to even get him to listen to me. God, that's a tempting picture."

Connor smiled. "He needs that lecture."

Dylan nodded. "If anyone could set him straight, it'd be you, Claire. You even scare Connor."

Connor's chest puffed. "I'm not afraid of Claire." Then he lowered his eyes. "I'm just grateful. Because of her, we don't embarrass Viviana anymore."

Aww. Claire smiled and touched his arm. They were more sensitive than they let on. "Connor, look at me." He raised his eyes. "I wish I had brothers like you and Dylan. Viviana was never embarrassed by you. Yes, she asked me to work with you, but do you know who else I work with?" She listed the names of several actors and musicians. "Anyone who wasn't raised with money needs a little guidance when they enter the world of those who were. It's a different culture, not better or worse, just different." When he didn't look sure of that, she added, "Grant said you taught him to fish. There's a lot he needed to learn when he entered your world. No one here is better than you."

Dylan snorted. "I'd like Ian to hear that."

"Hog-tie him for me sometime and I'll tell him," Claire joked and dropped her hand. "We should go back."

Connor and Dylan exchanged a look then said they had something to do first.

Claire shrugged. They'd held it together for the ceremony and most of the reception. Really, if they wanted to escape to a bar, who was she to judge?

As soon as she entered the reception hall, Annie waved to her from across the room. Seeing her friend, hand in hand with Kade, confident and absolutely glowing in a gorgeous floor-length wedding gown made everything else worth it.

A few months ago Annie and Kade had looked lost and unsure of themselves.

Coming to Boston to help them had been the right decision.

When a person did the right thing—things worked out. She had to believe that. In a better frame of mind, she began mingling and having fun again.

Later that evening, Claire's phone binged with a message from Dylan. He said he and Connor had something they wanted to give her. Could she meet them at her room?

How sweet. They're still worried about me.

They can't stand to see anyone upset.

I bet they got me flowers. Or took some from a vase at the reception. Claire smiled at the thought. *Either way, they mean well.*

The reception was winding down, so she didn't feel bad at all about ducking out again. Regardless of what they brought her, she was sure she'd love it.

Chapter Four

CURIOSITY WAS ALL that stopped Ian from instantly surging to his feet as soon as the laundry cart stopped and he regained his balance. He wanted to hear Claire's reaction—needed to know exactly what lay beneath her concerned best-friend persona. Then, and only then, would he show all three of them how foolish taking him on had been.

When the towel was whipped off his head he kept his hands tucked behind him. They didn't need to know he'd freed himself.

"One Ian Barrington—delivered exactly as you asked," Dylan announced.

"Hog-tied . . . well, duct-taped. Not sure if that's the same thing, but this is your chance, Claire."

Claire's eyes flew to Ian's and either she was a phenomenal actress or she was truly shocked. She swayed on her feet and her mouth dropped open. Ian held her gaze but didn't budge. *Show your true colors, Claire. Come on, let me see the real you.*

One of her hands went to her mouth while she pointed

at him with her other. "Oh, my God." Her face went white, bright pink, then white again. "Oh, my God." She bent and let out several audible breaths like she was hyperventilating. "Okay, think. Think." She turned to Dylan and Connor. "You two have to get out of here. Just go. I'll fix this."

The brothers looked from her to each other and back. Connor said, "We should stick around. He's not going to be happy when you take that tape off."

That is an understatement.

"I can handle him."

Oh, really?

She took several more deep breaths. "This is my fault. Oh, my God. You kidnapped Ian."

"Kidnapped? No," Dylan said dismissively. "That's illegal. This is more of a prank. You know, shit guys do to each other."

Prank? Ian's temper flamed. Still he didn't move. He was too fascinated by Claire's reaction.

She shook her head back and forth then started shoving Dylan and Connor toward the door. "Listen to me carefully. You both need to go back to your rooms and just lie low. Wait. No. Find Grant and Viviana. Don't tell them what you did, but stay where they can see you."

Just outside the door, Connor looked worried. "We went too far, didn't we? Do you want us to take Ian with us?"

"Take him? No. I've got this. Don't worry. It'll be fine." She closed the door and rested against it.

Okay, I'll play. I'm dying to see how you intend to smooth this over.

I can think of a few ways that might work. He pictured being restrained while she fucked him with her mouth. Or rode him until they both came. He'd love to tie her to his bed while he took her. Neither was his usual turn on, but when she came to stand in front of the laundry cart, chest still heaving, he also indulged in a quick fantasy of taking her over the rim of it. Tied up or free, there was a theme to his thoughts—her wrapped around him calling out his name as she came.

She bent down and reached out a hand toward the tape over his mouth. "Dylan and Connor didn't mean any harm. Think about Annie and Kade. No one wants their wedding day to end in an arrest. I'm going to take this off."

Their eyes met and she paused.

Hold on, could she be thinking what he was?

She frowned. "But before I do, I need to say something."

Apparently not.

She straightened and put her hands on her hips. "I feel horrible that this happened, but you need to know you're partly responsible. If you weren't such a complete asshole, I wouldn't have joked about wanting you hog-tied."

Her desire to see him restrained wasn't the same as his. *Shame, I was beginning to regret freeing myself.* His gaze fell to where the top of her gown was slipping lower and lower.

She followed his gaze, frowned again, then impatiently hauled the bodice of it higher. When their eyes met again, hers narrowed. "I'm serious. You should be nicer to Dylan and Connor. I'm leaving tomorrow, but they'll remain part of your family. Yes, they act before they think. Sure, they have more muscle than brains, but they made me feel welcomed from the first time I met them. All you did was walk around growling and glaring. Today is your brother's wedding and did you wear a smile to it? No. You were such a downer that Asher lectured you about it. *Asher.* If that's not a wake-up call, I don't know what is."

Her comments hit too close to home. He shifted his weight forward, preparing to remove the tape from his mouth and rise to his feet. Whatever amusement he might have found in the situation was gone right along with his boner.

She put a hand up for him to stop and continued her tirade. "I know you're angry. We all know that. Guess what? Life is not all about you and how you feel. You don't know what I'm going through. Why? Because you don't care enough to ask. I have my own shit I'm dealing with. I certainly didn't need the stress of you being delivered in a laundry cart. So, yes, I'm going to untie you, but first you'll promise you won't go to the police or do anything stupid because of this."

He made a sound behind the tape.

"Oh, I guess you can't promise anything with that on." She rubbed her forehead. "Nod once if you agree that this whole incident is better forgotten."

He let the coldness in his eyes be his answer.

She threw her hands up in the air. "Then, bring it on, I guess. I can't stop you from lashing out at everyone, but you don't have to be this angry all the time. Not everything is a tragedy. You might see that if you had a sense of humor."

He couldn't explain what held him immobile. The yearning in her voice? The openness of her gaze? In that moment, he saw himself through her eyes, and he didn't like the view.

That, of course, did not stop her from continuing to share her thoughts. "You can tell me it's none of my business. . ." She paused. "Actually, it's solely because you can't at this moment that I can be honest with you. I agree with Asher about Pamela. It doesn't matter what you find. You think you need the truth, but Annie and Kade are happy. Nothing you'd find is worth hurting them. I wish I could make you see that."

With a resigned expression she reached for his gag.

He caught her wrist, grabbed the corner of the tape with his other hand and swore as he tore it off. She struggled to free herself, but he held on as he rose to his feet and stepped out of the cart. Anger and desire muddled his ability to speak. "Stop," he barked.

Her eyes rounded. "You're not tied up."

His grip on her wrist tightened. "Can't get anything by you, can I?"

"Let go of me." Cheeks flushed. Eyes hot with the same desire that filled him. He didn't want this . . . didn't want to be tempted by those lips she was pressing together in anger. Just like, he was certain, she didn't want her nipples to tighten, proclaiming through the thin satin of her bridesmaid dress that she found this encounter equally exciting.

"Still certain you can handle me?" He pulled her closer. God, she smelled good.

She held his gaze. "You don't scare me. And if you hit me, you'd better kill me, because I'd get up . . . and when I did . . . you'd feel my fist as well."

Shock snapped his head back. "I would never raise a hand to a woman."

She looked down at his hold on her wrist. He instantly released her. "You're not a nice man, Ian Barrington. And, honestly, I don't know what you're capable of."

She sounded disgusted by him, but why did she look as turned on as he felt? He had to know if he was reading the situation wrong. So he leaned closer and in a low voice asked, "Then why do you want to fuck me?"

Without missing a beat, she answered, "I'm still trying to figure that out myself."

Her response echoed in him.

The first time because he was certain he'd misheard her.

The next because it mirrored how he felt.

He smiled. "You're not my type, Claire."

She rolled her eyes skyward and flipped her loosening hair. "You've made that abundantly clear."

"But I can't stop thinking about you. Whatever this is . . . it's some heady shit. What should we do about it?"

She stepped back and folded her arms protectively across herself. "Nothing. I go home tomorrow. The men waiting for me there are nice, normal guys."

"Men?" He didn't like the sound of that. "How many guys are in this Australian harem of yours?"

Her hands returned to her hips. "I didn't mean it like that and . . ." She made a frustrated sound. "I don't owe you any explanations. You and I are nothing to each other."

He leaned a little closer. "Oh, I see. You can stand in judgement of how I live my life, but I can't ask how many men you're running home to fuck."

"You're so . . . so crude."

His jaw tightened. "I am in a bit of a mood. I wonder what could have affected me . . . oh, wait, being duct taped, carried up twenty flights by a meathead, and stuffed into a—"

Her laughter took him completely by surprise, stopping him midsentence. "I'm sorry. I just pictured Dylan carrying you up the stairs."

"Connor. Dylan carried the cart."

A smile spread across her face and she gurgled as she tried to hold back another laugh. "I know it's not funny. I laugh when I'm nervous, and all I can picture is—"

He kissed her hand then closed the distance and claimed her mouth. He hadn't meant to. One second he was thinking she was beautiful when she smiled, then she was in his arms. It was a kiss that wasn't meant to be.

One that would have ended there, with that flash of sanity, had her arms not woven up around his neck. Had she not moaned and melted into his embrace.

Every inch of her fit against every inch of him like their bodies were made for this. He flicked a tongue over her lips, then deeper when she opened her mouth for him. So hot, so eager. He wanted—needed—more.

KISSING IAN SHOULDN'T have felt as right as it did. Months earlier, ever since their first touch, which had been his hand closing around hers in a firm handshake, she'd known he was dangerously tempting. He had done nothing to encourage the fantasies that had followed that initial meeting, but that had only made it more exciting.

Oh, yes, Ian Barrington had starred in an embarrassing number of her sexual fantasies where she was taken by a man she didn't like but desperately wanted. She'd even whispered his name once or twice while bringing herself to orgasm. Masturbation was a healthy alternative to sleeping around and a vivid go-to imaginary partner made abstinence that much easier.

This was different, though.

This was real.

Writhing against his excitement blew the socks off anything she'd imagined. She'd expected his touch to be rough, but there was skill rather than anger to the way he ran himself over her. Bold, strong, but in a controlled way. This was a man who knew how to fuck.

His tongue circled and teased.

His hands caressed and flirted with the parts of her that were ready and eager for his touch. His confidence was as insulting as it was electrifying.

He thinks the outcome of this is a done deal.

Without breaking off the kiss, he hiked her gown up and lifted her off the ground. Her legs naturally encircled his waist.

Because it is.

One hand cupped her ass, the other slid between them and slipped beneath the lace front of her thong. She moaned into his mouth when his fingers began to work their magic. Oh, no, this was no fumbling schoolboy. He knew exactly how to stroke her clit to turn off the warning bells in her head. The finger he slid inside her was thick with promise and gloriously knowledgeable about how to locate what other men found elusive.

Oh, God, yes.

Needing to feel more of him, she undid the buttons of his shirt then ran her hands over his muscled chest. She wanted to push his jacket off, but not if that required he move either of his hands.

When his mouth moved from hers to kiss its way down her neck, she clung to his shoulders from beneath his open shirt and threw her head back. Each kiss heated her skin, inching closer to the nipples she arched back farther to free.

Her reward was the wet heat of his tongue and the intense pleasure of his teeth scraping over her pulsing nub. If someone had told her she could be this ready this quickly, she wouldn't have believed them. Sex was something she'd enjoyed, but not when it was rushed. Her engines needed time to warm up.

Not with Ian. The finger he was pumping in and out of her sex quickly became not enough. She needed more of him. Craved all of him. She thrust herself forward, taking his finger deeper into herself and murmured, "Harder."

He slid another finger inside her and continued his adoration of her breasts. She closed her eyes and savored the feel of them. In and out, so perfectly in tune with the flick of his thumb over her clit. Heat rose within her. A beautiful, pure wave of pleasure that promised to take her even higher.

She swore when he withdrew his fingers.

Dammit, I was so close.

He strode forward. She clung to him, too far gone to care where he took her. She opened her eyes when her back hit the wall with a light thud and both of his hands encircled her bare ass. Pleasure and pain mixed when he lifted her higher. She splayed her arms out behind her to steady herself as he raised her sex to his lips.

Oh, yes.

Still wearing her high heels, she swung one leg over his shoulder, then the next.

He ripped her thong off in a move that both stung a little and excited her. He parted her sex with one hand and dove in with an enthusiasm that almost had her coming right then. It would have been so easy to give herself over to it, but she wanted the pleasure to last.

Sex had never been this kind of good.

And just in case it never was again, she sure as hell wasn't about to rush it.

His tongue teased her clit before rolling in and out of her. So thick. So hot. She dug one hand into his hair and held him where he was. If he stopped then she was certain she wouldn't survive.

In and out.

Back and forth.

Faster and deeper.

His breath a hot caress of its own.

He once again brought her to the brink.

The pleasure so intense it almost hurt.

Heat so pure she began to shake.

Then he stopped.

And she sobbed and tightened her hand in his hair. "Bastard."

She felt his chuckle against her sex. "Patience, Claire."

The sound of a condom package opening had her clenching her thighs around his head. She balanced herself as he undid his belt and opened his trousers. There was no question as to what was coming next or that this was all happening on his terms, but it was so good she didn't consider protesting.

The slight wall burn on her back she received from sliding back down him?

Worth it.

The bite of his belt into her thighs when she wrapped them back around his waist?

A good kind of pain.

And the taste of herself on his tongue when he plunged it back into her mouth?

The right kind of wrong.

In expectation of his pounding, she widened her legs for him.

His tip dipped in, withdrew, dipped in again.

Her control as well as her pride fell away. In hot whispers she begged him to take her. Begged him to fill her. His hands went to her hips, holding her still for the first powerful thrust that had her gasping and opening herself more for him.

"I knew you'd be a good fuck," he growled.

His declaration barely registered. She needed him deeper, wanted his mouth encircling her breasts again. She arched so she could have both.

With a growl, his control fell away, and he was taking her with the same abandon she felt. The power of his thrust was thrilling. The feel of him stretching her—addictive. She'd always known he had a larger than normal ego, but his equally impressive cock was a fulfilling bonus.

Using the wall behind her as leverage, he pounded into her. She wrapped herself around him, feverishly kissing any bare part of him she could reach . . . his neck, collarbone, one muscular pec.

Faster and faster.

Harder.

Deeper.

The heat that rose within her was stronger than either previous time. Like a surfer on a tsunami, she was helpless to do anything beyond riding it out. And ride it out, she did. She called out his name, louder and clearer than she had when this claiming had been in her mind alone. And when she came, she thought she might die from the intensity of it.

His pounding continued as she gave herself over to a shuddering, teary return to earth. One last powerful thrust. One growled swear and he joined her.

For a few long moments, neither moved as their breathing returned to normal. He pulled out and eased her back to her feet, an act that allowed her dress to fall around her ankles. He turned away, disposed of the condom in the trash near her bed and redid his belt. His shirt hung open beneath his tux jacket and his face was flushed.

Her sex was already humming for him again even as she fought to catch her breath. The silence dragged on, and his earlier words came back to her. "I knew you'd be a good fuck."

That's what this had been—a fuck.

It shouldn't have been better than the times she'd been with men she'd loved.

It should have felt dirty.

She definitely shouldn't want to strip and bed him for round two.

God, she wished he would say something instead of standing there looking as closed off to her as he'd always been. She'd just had mind-blowing, life-changing sex. How could he not have been as affected by what they'd shared?

She glanced down, realized the top of her gown was down around her waist, and pulled it up into place. Her gaze grazed over the front of his trousers and lingered on the growing evidence that he wanted more as well.

When she raised her eyes to his again, time stood still.

No matter who they had been before this or who they would be later, right then they were simply two people who were still hungry for each other. His nostrils flared. She quivered in anticipation.

He looked like he was also searching for what to say. Was there anything either of them could say that wouldn't take away from the moment? She didn't think so.

His voice was deep and husky when he said, "Claire—"

A loud knock on the hotel door cut off what he would have said. "Claire? It's Viviana and Grant. Is Ian still with you?"

How Ian had come to be in her room in the first place came rushing back, and Claire bent over, hands on her knees, gasping for air as a panic attack took hold. She hadn't had one in years and had thought herself beyond them, but as this one took hold so did a deeper fear that she was one more mistake away from becoming her mother.

Ian was at her side, bending so his face was level with hers. "Are you okay?"

She shook her head back and forth. She felt many things in that moment, but okay wasn't one of them. Deep breath. Deep breath. Deep breath. Deep breath. Mind over body. *I'm not having a heart attack. My airway isn't actually blocked. I'm doing this to myself.* Deep breath. Deep breath.

Slowly she brought her mind as well as her body back under her control.

Grant's voice boomed through the door. "Ian, open the door."

"How do you expect him to when he's tied up?" Viviana's question floated through the door.

"I doubt he still is," Grant said with confidence. "But if he's in there, he'd better say so now."

Grant sounded so angry that Claire teetered on losing it again, but instead pointed to the bathroom. "You have to hide."

"I don't hide," Ian said with such a lack of emotion, Claire wanted to smack him.

Oh, my God. She kept her voice low. "Listen, I don't normally eat carbs. Zero. None. But I'm ten pounds heavier because I broke that rule in Boston. Chaos doesn't just happen. It requires one bad choice after another. I've made my share of them lately. I've alienated my clients, put on weight, participated in a kidnapping, had sex with a man I don't like. I'm not blaming you for any of it, but I'm asking you . . . okay, begging you to help me stop this from becoming more of a train wreck. Hide in the bathroom, the closet, under the bed. I don't care. Just don't let them find you here looking like . . ."

She waved a hand at his open shirt.

"Right," he said and spun on his heel, disappearing into the bathroom.

"One minute," Claire called out. She looked around, spotted her torn thong on the floor and kicked it under the bed, then checked her dress in the mirror over the dresser and walked to the door. *You can do this. Just breathe.* She forced a smile and opened the door. "Viviana. Grant."

Frowning, Grant walked past her to the laundry cart where the discarded pieces of duct tape still lay. "Where's Ian?"

"You were right, Claire, the soap took the glue from the tape right off." Ian emerged from the bathroom with his shirt buttoned and pristinely tucked back in his trousers. "Oh, Grant. Come to save me? You're a bit late."

Viviana joined Grant. "Ian, I'm so sorry about my brothers. When they told us what they'd done—"

"Don't give it a second thought," Ian said smoothly.

Grant gave him a long look. "You're not angry?"

"I was," Ian pocketed his hands and rolled his shoulders. "I'm over it."

Viviana looked back and forth from Claire to Ian. Ian held her gaze with seeming ease, Claire cursed the blush that spread up her neck.

"What am I missing?" Grant asked.

Finding her voice, Claire said, "Nothing. After Viviana's brothers left I released Ian and we had a good laugh over it. Right Ian?" Her eyes riveted to his and she silently pleaded him to go along with her.

A hint of a smile curled a corner of his mouth. "That's what we had—a good—*laugh*."

"You are handling this so much better than I thought you would," Grant said slowly.

Ian's gaze met Claire's again briefly, then he said, "What can I say? I like to *laugh*, and I had no idea how funny Claire could be."

Claire's cheeks warmed. It was impossible to be so close to Ian and not remember how he tasted, crave more from that talented tongue of his. She wiped a hand over her forehead. "All's well that ends well, right?"

Ian bent and growled into her ear, "Oh, this is not the end."

Claire elbowed him sharply in the side. "Since you're here, Grant, maybe you and Ian could return that cart before someone misses it."

Ian looked about to protest when Viviana stepped farther into the room and said, "Go ahead, Grant. I'm sure Ian needs a drink after this ordeal. I'll stay with Claire."

"Come on, Ian, you deserve that drink. Thank you for understanding that Dylan and Connor were only trying to help." Grant clapped a hand on Ian's shoulder.

There wasn't much he could do, so his nod of acceptance didn't come as a surprise. He exchanged one last long look with Claire, followed Grant out of the hotel room, and closed the door behind him. Only then did Claire sag and take a seat on the edge of her bed.

Viviana came to sit beside her. "I thought you didn't like Ian."

Me too. "I don't dislike him. He's just so—" She normally would have described him as insufferably arrogant and negative, but those weren't the words that came to mind when she thought of him now. Forceful, passionate, mysterious. She swallowed hard.

"The two of you look good together."

Claire leaned back onto her hands. "We're not together."

"Oh, I just thought maybe having him delivered to your room might have led to—"

"It didn't." Normally Claire didn't approve of lying, but there was nothing normal about this situation.

"I had sex with Grant in a supply closet the first day we met. I'm not here to judge you, Claire. The heart wants what the heart wants."

Claire brought both of her hands up to cover her face for a moment, before dropping them to her lap. "Did you really sleep with Grant the first day you met?"

"There was no sleep involved," Viviana said with a smile

and wink. "You and Ian have been circling each other for weeks. Just tell me we didn't interrupt. Grant was worried Ian would be furious. I had faith that you could handle him if he was."

Laughing only because she didn't know what else to do, Claire said, "I still can't believe we . . . you know . . . he kept saying I wasn't his type."

Viviana wrinkled her nose. "Men—especially Barrington men—have a hard time unraveling their feelings. What about you? How was it?"

There was no use denying what she already knew. "Great. Better than great. It doesn't mean anything, though. I go home tomorrow."

Viviana stood. "Want my advice?"

Why not. "Sure."

"Leave tonight. Right now."

"Run away?"

"Fly actually. I can have a plane ready for you in thirty minutes. Annie and Kade are already off on their honeymoon. If you stay, Ian will be back here tonight."

"And that would be a problem?" Claire wasn't the type to run away. Sure, having sex with Ian again probably was a bad idea, but she should at least stay long enough to talk about what they'd done. Shouldn't she?

"I guess it depends if you're looking for just sex or marriage."

"Hang on a minute." Claire raised her hand. "First, I have a life I love in Australia. I have a career I worked hard to build and friends. I don't need a man to complete me. I'm already happy."

"Okay."

"And if I were looking for a relationship, it wouldn't be with someone like Ian. People think relationships can make them happy, but happiness comes from within. No one can make another person happy. Just like they can't make them miserable. We decide how we feel. I can't fix him."

"You're right."

"I know I am."

"I still think you should fly out tonight."

Claire searched Viviana's face. "Why?"

Viviana clapped her hands and chucked her shoulder into Claire's. "Because we all want you to marry Ian. Imagine how perfect that would be. Annie would be thrilled. Sophie and Dale already consider you one of their children. You could move here, and we could all raise the next generation together."

"Wow. I'm not looking to get married."

"But you're not *not* looking to get married, are you?"

Claire let that roll around in her head before answering. "I'm not against the idea of marriage—between two compatible people. I barely know Ian, but what I do know is that we have nothing in common."

Still smiling, Viviana said, "What *I know* is that my brothers manhandled Ian and escaped without repercussion. More than that? When Ian was looking at you he did something I didn't think he was capable of—he smiled. You might not think that's a big deal, but the whole family is worried about him. They're afraid he's fixating on something that will tear them apart again. Okay, maybe you can't fix him, but you could pull him back from the brink of a mistake he won't be able to undo. You could give him something else to think about besides what happened thirty years ago."

"You're asking me to use sex to manipulate him?"

Viviana chewed her bottom lip and made a face. "It didn't sound as bad as that in my head."

Does Viviana realize that sometimes she sounds just like her brothers?

"I won't do it." *There. I can't be clearer than that.*

Wrinkling her nose again, Viviana stood. "The one thing all the Barrington men have in common is they've had it too easy when it comes to getting the women they want. They're rich. They're gorgeous. Women throw themselves at them—even after they're married. All that attention is not good for them. You might want to consider that giving Ian's ego a little trim would actually be doing him a favor. He'd be a kinder, humbler version of himself for whichever woman does decide to marry him."

After this talk, Claire did want to leave, but not to help Ian prepare himself for a relationship with another woman. And not in hopes that it would initiate a chase that would lead him to propose to her.

She wanted the craziness of this trip to end and to step back into her own life. She wanted to start eating better, rebuild her clientele, and forget about how good sex could be with the wrong person.

It meant leaving without talking things out with Ian, but

she doubted talking was what he would return with hopes of—so maybe leaving was for the best.

"How soon can you have that plane readied?"

"You will not regret this," Viviana said before throwing her arms around Claire and giving her a tight hug.

"That's my goal."

Chapter Five

DOWN IN THE hotel bar with Grant, Ian took a sip of bourbon the bartender handed him. Alcohol was not what he was craving. He didn't want to be impaired at all when he returned to Claire's room.

The evening sure had taken an unexpected turn, but a surprisingly pleasurable one. Normally, he kept his sex life completely separate from his family. Claire broke that rule by being dangerously intertwined with his brother's new wife.

Intertwined. He smiled as the word brought his more intimate connection to her to mind. Some things were worth breaking a few rules for.

Grant's voice broke in. "Too bad Dylan and Connor waited until after the ceremony to kidnap you."

Ian shook his head to refocus his attention on his brother. "Excuse me?"

"This is the happiest you've looked in a while—especially today. Mom was half-afraid you were going to stand up and protest the union."

"Why would she think that? I approve of Annie. She's good for Kade."

"You're hiding that well." Grant laid his still half-full glass of bourbon on the bar and arched an eyebrow at Ian. "She's worried about you, Ian. We all are."

"Me? Why?"

"Discovering Kade was still alive hasn't been easy on any of us. It's ripped open the past, and the experience has been understandably unsettling."

"If there's something you need to talk out—talk. However, if this conversation is for my benefit, don't bother. I've already reached capacity for all I can stomach on the subject."

"Nothing that happened back then was your fault."

Ian downed the rest of his drink without responding.

Grant continued, "Dad believed the doctors. We believed Dad. There was no reason to look for someone we'd buried."

Feeling cornered, Ian growled, "What part of 'I don't want to talk about this' are you having trouble understanding?"

Grant swirled his glass before saying, "You've always been on the right side of the fight, Ian. Our family wouldn't be where we are today if not for you. You cleaned up every mess Asher made. You might think I don't know how you've covered my back when my competitors came for me, but I do. You were always the first one to nag us to gather whenever Mom needed us. There is so much good in you—but not much of that is showing lately. You're becoming someone I don't recognize, so yes I'm going to talk about it . . . even if you don't want to."

Ian rubbed a hand over his forehead. Grant was a quiet voice of reason in a storm of emotion. Like a beacon in the distance, his brother's concern called to him, but Ian couldn't change course. "I need to know what happened back then," he said in a low, guttural voice. "I know it wasn't my fault, but there were so many signs I should have seen. So many things I missed. I can't drop it. The frustration of not knowing is what you see in my face—not disapproval of Kade or Annie."

Grant sighed. "And when you find your answers?" He placed his glass back on the bar. "What then?"

"I don't know," Ian admitted.

"You can't hurt Pamela without destroying Kade. To him, she will always be his mother. If you keep digging, you might find something. God help us if you do, because if that's where this goes, you won't be on the right side anymore, and I won't be able to stand with you."

Grant was the numbers guy in their family. Normally he was all about uncomfortable truths. This was a whole different level of uncomfortable, though. Grant was becoming their father, and not in a way Ian could stomach. Their father had taught them to hide what they felt. The illusion of perfection was more important than the reality. As long as he could remember, Ian had been encouraged to not ask, not see.

Ian would never understand why it had been so easy for their father to accept the loss of Kade when a little digging would have brought him back as an infant. *Are you all so afraid that you need to rewrite history and pretend the last thirty years weren't hell for our family? I can't do that.*

I won't do that. The bartender shouldn't have refilled Ian's glass because he downed that in one gulp. "Then I'd better not find anything."

Grant downed the rest of his drink as well. Neither spoke. There wasn't anything else to say.

A short while later, slightly buzzed, Ian stood at the elevator of the hotel without pressing the call button. He was conflicted. Part of him wanted nothing more than to return to Claire and spend the rest of the night in the blissful distraction of her arms. Another part of him didn't want to bring his sour mood to her.

He considered texting her, but when he took out his phone to do so, no words came to him.

He'd told her he didn't trust her. She couldn't be expecting anything meaningful to come from what they'd done.

Had Grant and Viviana not interrupted their time together—how would the rest of the evening have gone?

More sex definitely.

But then?

He didn't want more than that from her.

Still, he couldn't just leave her there waiting for him to return. He called for the elevator, stepped into it when it arrived, and pressed the button for her floor.

She didn't answer his first knock, so he knocked again . . . harder. "Claire, it's Ian."

Nothing.

He knocked again.

Had she gone out?

Perhaps headed downstairs to look for him?

He was about to turn away, when another door opened and Viviana stuck her head out of her room. "Oh, Ian. Are you looking for Claire?"

Difficult to deny it when he was standing at her door. "Yes."

"She's gone."

"Gone?"

"Left for the airport a little while ago. She was supposed to leave tomorrow but seemed anxious to get home so I arranged a flight for her."

He frowned.

Anxious to get home? She hadn't looked upset when he'd left her? He didn't like the idea that she might have been. "Was she—did she look—?" He stopped.

"She seemed fine. My guess is she has someone waiting for her back in Australia. She gave up a lot to help Annie and Kade. Nearly two months. That can't have been good for her business or for her relationships. I hope she's able to get both back on track."

"Did she mention someone?" He gritted his teeth briefly after the words left his mouth. He told himself he didn't care if she did. She could already be back and fucking every man in Australia for all he cared. She was nothing to him.

"No one specifically. She's such a great person, though, I can't imagine her not fighting off a bunch of suitors. Beautiful. Intelligent. Successful. And so nice. I hope whoever he is likes Boston and doesn't mind large families. Your parents practically consider Claire one of their own. If she returns with someone, your parents will probably insist they stay with them."

Never. Going. To. Happen.

"Good night, Viviana," Ian said in a curt voice.

"Good night, Ian." Viviana sounded too pleased with herself for Ian not to realize she'd had an agenda when she'd opened her door.

He'd been warned the women of the family were hoping he and Claire would hook up. Could the whole night have been set up with that in mind?

No.

They wouldn't go that far.

Would they?

He remembered telling Asher he couldn't be taken by surprise, but Dylan and Connor had proved that wrong. If his family had orchestrated the whole evening, they'd be disappointed to discover their plan hadn't worked.

The sex had been good. So what?

Better than it had been with anyone in a while.

Maybe ever.

So, sure he was disappointed she was gone, but it was better for both of them that she was.

One good fuck didn't mean he had any claim to her.

It didn't mean he'd changed his opinion of her in the slightest.

After letting himself into his hotel suite, he kicked the door shut behind him.

The taste of her was still on his lips.

The scent of her still on his clothing.

He stripped down, tossing his clothing in a pile near his bed while trying to block out an image of how she would have looked on his bed. After a long, cold shower, he lay in that bed, cursing her for lingering in his thoughts.

When his phone beeped with a message, he lunged for it then cursed again when he saw it was only a message from his brother Lance asking him if he was okay. He tossed the phone aside without answering it.

I shouldn't have had sex with her. I told myself not to. I knew it was a bad idea.

He folded his hands behind his head and tried to remember if she'd ever mentioned a man's name. Back when he'd first heard about her, he'd had one of his good friends perform a full background check on her. Bradford had also investigated some of the men her name had been linked with. A movie star. A politician. A pro soccer player. Annie claimed they were just Claire's clients.

Clients?

Is that what they called fuck buddies in Australia?

Chapter Six

A WEEK LATER Claire was sitting in her Melbourne office with her feet on her desk and an empty bag of potato chips in front of her. The bottom of her coffee cup was uncharacteristically covered with sugar residue. Her phone messages were full of texts from her personal yoga instructor asking her if she'd returned yet, friends wanting to meet up for drinks, and two men she'd dated before leaving for the US . . . one she hadn't slept with yet, one she had. Sadly she had no interest in seeing either of them again.

I could go for a brownie, though.

God, I haven't had one of those in years.

Her phone buzzed with a call from Sophie Barrington. Claire let it go to voice mail. Never in her life had she imagined she would be the type to hide, but that's what she was doing.

Hiding and silently freaking the fuck out.

So far, every single client she'd contacted had moved on for one reason or another. Everything she'd built. Everything she'd been proud of was . . . *poof*—gone as if it hadn't existed. She tried to tell herself she was overreacting, choosing negative thoughts when positivity was the only path to success.

Her phone buzzed again. Sophie. No one could accuse the matriarch of the Barrington clan of giving up. Seriously, she was also the sweetest woman, and Claire felt too guilty to not pick up again. "Hi, Sophie."

"It's late here which I think means it's morning there. I hope I didn't wake you."

"You didn't. I'm already at my office. What can I do for you?"

"Nothing. This morning Dale and I were saying how much we miss you. It was truly wonderful having you stay with us while you were here. We want you to know that you're welcome anytime."

"I miss you too. And thank you." Tears misted Claire's eyes. What would it have been like to have been raised by such a mother? Claire reached for another potato chip before remembering that she'd already finished the last of them.

"You left so fast I was worried something had happened. We'd hoped to see you one last time."

"Something came up—" She stopped because lying to someone like Sophie felt wrong. "No. It didn't. I'm sorry. I just felt like I needed to be back home."

"I can imagine it must have been difficult to be away for as long as you were. Don't think your sacrifice went unnoticed. We are so grateful you came over to support Kade and Annie."

"There was no sacrifice . . ."

"So your company is booming?"

Sophie couldn't know how empty her calendar was, could she? "Things always happen when you look away from your business, but it's nothing I can't handle."

"I have connections even in Australia. If you have openings, I can mention you to my friends."

Claire's pride kicked in as she remembered what Ian had said about her wanting to link her name with his family. It was never about that. "Thank you, but you don't have to do that."

"I realize I don't have to, but—"

"Please don't, Sophie."

After a quiet moment, Sophie said, "Annie and Kade are gone on their honeymoon. Pamela and Dave are on a tour of New England with Clay and Lexi. Are you sure you're okay? I hate the idea of you being alone."

"I'm not alone. This is where my life is."

"Something is wrong."

"Nothing is wrong." *Nothing I can't figure out.*

"Then could we FaceTime?"

"Uh—"

"It's so difficult to read someone over the phone. Better than texting, but not like seeing them in person. Just look me in the eye and tell me I'm worrying over nothing and I'll believe you."

Blinking back tears, Claire cracked. "I messed up, Sophie. But not so badly that I can't fix it. It'll just take time." She pushed the empty bag of chips away. "I'm angry with myself for not being perfect and punishing myself for it. That's all you'd see if you looked into my eyes. Nothing tragic. Nothing that will last. I'm just basking in the stupidity of my mistakes."

"We've all been there. I knew you were struggling with something. Doesn't it feel better to share the weight of it?"

"Yes and no. I'm used to handling things on my own." While she was being honest . . . "It's scary to let anyone in."

"Not just anyone. We're like family now."

It was a nice thought, but not true. "I'm just Annie's friend."

"Family isn't only by blood. And I'm not going anywhere. I know it's hard for you to trust that, so I'll just have to prove it to you. If your mother were still alive I would have a few choice words for her."

"She wouldn't have listened to you, either," Claire said in a kneejerk reaction, then regretted saying anything bad about her mother. She didn't usually talk about her past with anyone, not like she'd shared with Sophie, but the woman had a way of wearing a person's defenses down. This, though, was the first harsh thing Claire had ever heard Sophie say—about anyone.

"I'm sorry. I've made my own share of mistakes, I just wish she had treasured you."

Me too.

But we don't always get what we want, do we?

Claire kept her thoughts to herself because Sophie had never been anything but wonderful to her. Any anger Claire had left in her was for someone who could never make it up to her anyway.

Sophie continued, "Okay, so you've made some mistakes. Any that Annie is aware of?"

Sophie belonged in the CIA. No secrets were safe around her. "No."

"Then it's settled. Dale and I are coming to Melbourne for a mini vacation. We'll take you out to dinner, talk through whatever mess you've gotten yourself into and be home before anyone even notices. No one will be the wiser, and we'll have you right back on track. Where do you suggest we stay?"

"You don't have to do that. I'm fine, really."

"It's done. Claire, I have wasted too much time wishing I could do something but being afraid to take the next step and simply do it. You have been so good to us. Let me return some of that kindness."

"You don't even know what the problem is."

"No, but I know you and that whatever you're dealing with is something that you don't have to go through alone."

Even with Annie, Claire had been the strong one . . . the one with the answers. Was it so wrong to want someone to talk this out with? "All I'll accept is advice."

"That's fair enough. While we're on that subject, have you been doing yoga since you've been back? I remember you saying you enjoyed it."

Claire's eyes widened and she looked around her office, half expecting to see a camera on her. *If she tells me to stop indulging in chips, I'll worry.* "I haven't yet."

"Do some today. I have a feeling it's just what you need. And don't forget to send us a suggestion for where we should stay. Somewhere quiet. After all the excitement of the wedding, it'll be nice to unwind. I have to speak to Dale, but I'd say we'll be there in about two days. Who knows, we may try out Annie's new international jet service. Keep her employees on their toes while she's away."

"I'll find you a place today." She almost ended the call there, but had to ask, "Sophie, did Viviana talk to you?"

"About?"

"Anything."

"Was there something in particular she should have? Or *shouldn't* have?"

Leaning back in her chair, Claire absently scanned the ceiling. "No. I just want to make sure you're not coming here because you think—"

"What are you worried I might think?"

I can't imagine Viviana telling Sophie that I slept with Ian. "Nothing. I'm still processing that you want to come see me." She swallowed hard. "How did you know I was struggling?"

"A mother always knows," Sophie said gently.

Not all mothers.

Mine never saw how much her lifestyle affected me.

Or she never cared enough to put my needs before her own.

I really don't know.

"I'll have everything ready for when you arrive, Sophie."

After hanging up, Claire walked to the window of her office and stared blindly out at the view of the city she'd once considered all she needed. Annie had always been the sister she'd never had. She'd told herself she didn't need parents. Even Annie's parents, nice as they'd been, hadn't changed her mind.

My mother wasn't a bad person, just a selfish one.

As the result of sex with a man whose name her mother couldn't remember, Claire had been a surprise her mother hadn't embraced. She'd loved Claire, but she'd been young and hadn't wanted to change her wild lifestyle. So her mother had floated from relationship to relationship, taking Claire with her like an afterthought. When her mother drank she'd been impulsive. Claire never knew where she would be sleeping or if her mother would stay in the same home with her. She didn't know if the man they were staying with would greet her with a smile or throw her things out along with her mother's.

When Claire became too much for her mother to handle, she sent her to live with her grandmother, and that's where Annie had come into her life. Her mother had been free to go off and live her wild life while Claire had done her best to piece herself back together after hearing her grandmother tell a neighbor she was too old to want to raise another child.

It was just me after that. In every way that mattered.

Claire had moved away as soon as she'd been able to, and she'd put all that behind her. She'd gone to therapy and talked herself in circles until she'd picked herself up, shaken herself off, and redefined herself.

She was strong now.

Confident.

The little girl who'd desperately wanted a family had grown up and let that dream go. She glanced back at her desk and made a face at the bag of chips and sweet coffee she wouldn't have allowed herself before Boston.

This isn't about Ian.

Or my elusive clients.

This is about me.

For two months she'd been part of a family. Game nights. Bickering. Children everywhere. She'd always told herself she was better off alone, but staying with the Barringtons had stirred something inside her.

I do want a family—the kind that doesn't leave. The kind that understands love isn't a burden.

I don't want to be alone.

An image of Ian came to her, but she shook her head. *No. He would have been my mother's type. She had a thing for lost causes.*

Look how that turned out for her.

She overdosed alone.

That doesn't have to be my life, though. My choices aren't an arrogant asshole or a solitary existence.

Ian is nothing to me.

I'm sure sex can be just as good with a nice man. Someone who cares about someone besides himself.

Ian won't be happy when he finds out his mother is coming to see me.

Guess what, Mr. Gloomy Pants? I really don't care how you feel about anything.

THE NEXT MORNING Ian was not in a good mood when he sprinted up the steps of his parents' home. It wasn't unusual for him to start his day by calling his family. What was unusual was that morning neither of his parents had picked up. His next call had been to Grant to ask if he'd heard from them. Dale's health had become more and more of a concern over the past year, and after finding him on the floor a few months ago, Ian didn't take a day with him for granted.

Grant hadn't sounded concerned. "When I spoke to Mom about an hour ago she said they were flying out this afternoon."

"Where are they going?" It was the first Ian had heard of them planning a trip anywhere. "Who is going with them?" Their father's recent collapse had been the result of him accidentally overmedicating himself; the idea of them heading off anywhere alone was unsettling.

"No one as far as I know, unless you're volunteering."

"They shouldn't travel alone."

"Dad hasn't had an episode in months. I offered to go with, but Mom said they don't need a babysitter."

"And you accepted that?" An idea came to him that calmed him somewhat. If Grant wasn't worried, it probably meant their parents were not going that far. "Are they heading to Nantucket?"

"Melbourne."

"Australia? Why would they go there while both Kade and Annie are in the US?" His gut clenched. Was it possible his parents were looking into the truth of Kade's disappearance as well? "What do you know that you're not saying, Grant?"

"Go see Mom and Dad yourself. It's better coming from them."

Ian would have demanded Grant spill what he knew if Grant had not already terminated the call. Whatever, he had already cleared his schedule for the wedding and hadn't yet chosen his next project.

His father opened the door before Ian knocked. Although his parents could afford staff, they lived a modest lifestyle—at least by the standards of their peers. Sure they only flew on private planes, but Dale wheeled his own luggage. No amount of telling him it wasn't necessary would change his mind, either. His father prided himself on staying humble, grounded, and kind.

It was a code of living that hadn't served Dale or their family well.

Along with his youngest son, Dale had lost his political career, most of his personal fortune, and almost his wife. His children had suffered in silence, in constant fear that something they may say or do might prove too much for their fragile mother.

Dale struggled with regret.

As he should.

He knew Mom's sister was dangerous.

He should have protected his career—more importantly his wife and children—from Patrice.

Being a good person only works when dealing with those of the same moral code. Unfortunately, the world was full of people who could lie as easily as they could breathe. They steal. They betray. They kidnap.

If Patrice's orders had been followed, Kade would have been murdered the night he'd been taken. It was an ugly truth no one wanted to face. As was the question of Pamela's involvement. Why she'd chosen to run to Australia with Kade was a nagging mystery to Ian. She said to protect him. She claimed to not have known who he was, but she'd worked at the clinic Kade had been taken from. She knew too many of the players to not have had access to the truth of who he was. It was far more likely she'd either been involved from the start and gotten cold feet or had her own brother killed for his cut of the money and had used Kade as a way to convince Dave to take her back . . . therefore providing her with the perfect place to hide.

All Ian had to do was find a money trail.

Or someone connected to the incident who was still alive.

Neither was proving easy to do.

"Ian, what a surprise," his father said with a welcoming smile.

Ian walked through the open door. "It wouldn't be one if you'd answered your phone. I called both you and Mom—then Grant. You had me worried."

His father closed the door behind him. "Well, as you can see, we're fine. Sophie must have packed my phone already. You know how your mother is. She has a list, and once it gets checked off, I don't dare touch anything."

"Is that Ian?" Sophie called out from the kitchen.

"Yes, he's here to lecture us about not answering our phones," Dale called back with amusement. "I blamed you."

"Shocking," his mother joked back. "Who wants coffee? I just made a fresh pot."

A moment later, in the kitchen, Ian looked both of his parents over with a critical eye and conceded that they looked fine. His father's health seemed to have stabilized. His mother still had the glow that had returned to her the day she'd learned Kade was alive.

His father hadn't stopped smiling since Kade had set foot back in Boston.

Sophie cupped Ian's face in greeting. "Are you sleeping? You look tired."

He laid his hand over his mother's and gave it a gentle squeeze. "I'm fine, Mom. You did age me a little, though, when neither of you picked up this morning."

After lowering her hands slowly, his mother searched his face. "It's not like you to spend so much time in Boston. Is anything going on you want to talk about?"

"I'm on a short break." Raising his head, Ian stepped back. "But there is something I want to discuss. Why do you and Dad want to go to Australia? Everyone is here."

His father handed Ian a cup of black coffee. Ian accepted it and leaned back against the kitchen counter. His parents exchanged a look.

"I enjoyed our time there," his mother said in a cheerful tone.

His father added, "Annie's fleet makes it an easy choice. Besides, not everyone is here. We intend to visit with Claire in Melbourne. She found us a rental in a great area. We—"

"No. Every part of this is a bad idea." Ian slammed his coffee onto the counter beside him.

His father cleared his throat. "We're going."

Drumming his fingers on the counter on either side of him, Ian heard the slight reprimand in his father's tone, but it wasn't enough to stop him. "Did Claire ask you to go see her?" When neither of his parents answered immediately, he pushed, "What does she want? Money? Introductions to your connections? Tell me exactly what she said when she asked you to go."

Dale handed Sophie a mug of coffee. "Do you remember when we used to grill Ian on where he was going and who he planned to spend his time with? Did you ever think we'd be on the other side of that talk?"

Sophie wrapped her hands around the mug and chuckled. "I do recall him once saying he was old enough to do as he pleased, and we needed to learn to trust him. We could try that."

"That was Asher." Ian arched a brow. "And I'm serious."

With a light of amusement in his eyes, his father leaned closer to his mother. "He's serious. Better watch or we'll be sent to our rooms."

"That's not a threat to anyone over the age of thirty, is it?" His mother's laugh rang out. "I quite enjoy a midday nap."

Ian sighed and crossed his arms over his chest. Yes, it was nice to see his parents in a good mood, but there was no way in hell they were flying off to see Claire . . . jokes or no jokes. "When I spoke to you yesterday neither of you mentioned this trip."

"We just decided to go." Dale put an arm around Sophie's waist. "It was actually your mother's idea, but I didn't have a chance to see Melbourne while we were there, and it'll be nice to see Claire again."

"Claire." Ian said her name between gritted teeth.

Dale studied his son's face. "I wasn't aware you had an issue with her. Did something happen?"

Ian wasn't touching that one. "No. I just don't trust her."

Dale shrugged. "That's a shame because your mother and I adore her. We were hoping the two of you would hit it off, but it looks like we'll have to adopt her instead." The twinkle in his father's eye did nothing to improve Ian's mood.

"Don't encourage Ian," Sophie said. "He's not what Claire needs. She belongs with someone who—"

"Who?" Ian prompted even as his mother was still speaking.

She met his gaze. "Someone who will treasure her. She hasn't had it easy."

It sounded to Ian like Claire had played on his mother's heartstrings. It was nothing more than he should have expected. "Have you considered she may be living exactly the life she deserves?"

Dale nodded. "I see your point, Sophie. Ian wouldn't be good for Claire. Alessandro might know someone who would, though. Once she's back on her feet, plant the idea in his head that he should find someone for her, and she'll be happily married by Christmas."

Nodding, his mother's smile returned. "He really has become a master matchmaker. I'll give him a call when we return."

There wasn't a part of the conversation Ian was enjoying. He didn't like the idea that Claire might be manipulating his parents into helping her. He also didn't enjoy imagining her happily married to another man.

The second realization elicited a frustrated growl. He didn't want her so the idea of her with another man shouldn't bother him. It was annoying that it did. "You're not going to Melbourne."

The surprise on both of his parents' faces would have been comical had it been for any other reason. Sophie stepped toward him and placed a hand on his arm. "We love you, Ian. Your concern for us is heartwarming. Truly, it makes me proud that I have raised a son who feels so protective of his parents." She gave his arm a light squeeze. "Now, look me in the eye and listen carefully. Your father and I don't require your permission to do anything. If you'd like to come with us, you're welcome. Would you like to come with us?"

"No," he ground out but wavered in the face of the strength he saw in his mother's eyes. They'd always thought she was the fragile one, but they'd underestimated her. She'd faltered beneath the weight of Kade's disappearance, but somehow she'd come out the other side the strongest of them all. "Yes. I'll have my things brought to the airport."

Sophie glanced back at Dale. "He doesn't trust us not to go without him."

For the first time that day there was a hint of sadness in his father's eyes. "Understandable. Trust is earned, and I let him down."

Sophie took Dale's hand in hers. "No, you didn't. You made the best choices you knew how to at every step. What more can we expect from each other?"

He hugged her to his chest. "Your love is more than I deserve, but I'll happily spend the rest of my life trying to live up to whatever you see in me."

"I love you too, Dale. No matter what life throws at us, that has never wavered." Sophie smiled up at her husband then across to Ian. "Claire deserves someone who can love her that way. Alessandro is a good judge of character. I'll ask him to find someone he could see fitting into our family. I know it's selfish of me, but once she and Annie start having babies I'd love to have them both stateside."

Ian's chest tightened and a vein in his forehead began to pulse. The number of people planted around the world who would act without question on his command was substantial, but none of them happened to share his last name. Returning to Australia at this time had not been in his plans, but perhaps his investigation into the past needed to expand to other people in Pamela's circle. Claire was too young to have been involved, but she might know something—have overheard something—or her mother, the one who had died from an overdose, might have come to a sinister ending because of her own involvement.

It was a stretch for sure, but every part of Kade's kidnapping would be considered the same.

The problem with uncovering a lie such as the one that had rocked through his family was determining how deep those lies went.

And then there was Claire. She wanted something.

Hopefully his presence alone would be enough to make her think twice before messing with his family.

Chapter Seven

THE NEXT DAY, on the tarmac of a private airport just outside of Melbourne, Claire ran her cold hands down the sides of her knee-length skirt. She was excited to see Sophie and Dale again. It was important to her that everything about their visit went smoothly.

There was no media present when Sophie and Dale arrived. Two SUVs stood ready—one for all of them to ride in to the rental—the other to send their luggage ahead. It would be unpacked and stored by the time they pulled into the driveway, but the driver knew to allow Dale to pack his bags into the back himself.

From living with them, Claire knew the temperature to set the rental air conditioner to. She'd stocked the fridge and pantry with doctor-approved versions of their favorite foods. A chef and house staff were on call but would not be visible unless paged.

Plans had already been made for Sophie and Dale to have lunch the next day with Annie's parents, Mitch and Hazel. If things went the way Claire anticipated, Sophie and Dale would spend the next few days having a relaxing visit.

When the plane door opened, Sophie stepped out with Dale just behind her. He placed his bag down to wave. Sophie also waved when she spotted her. Warmth filled Claire's soul. The love she saw in their faces had her fighting back happy tears. Family. This was how having one was supposed to feel.

Dale stepped forward, tripped over his bag, and stumbled down a few stairs.

Oh, my God.

Claire instantly set off in a high-heeled run. Shaking, he was holding onto the railing by the time Claire made it to the base of the stairs.

Sophie was at his side. "Easy there, Dale. You're okay. This is the part of our lives when we're supposed to stop flying."

He smiled, but it didn't reach his eyes. "That first step was a doozy."

"Are you okay?" Claire asked in a rush. "Did you hurt anything?"

With his hand still gripping the railing, he shook his head. "Just my pride."

"Dad?" Ian took the stairs two at time. If looks could kill, Claire would not have survived the one he gave her as he laid a steadying hand on his father's shoulder. "What happened?"

Ian.

Claire swayed on her feet.

Intimate memories of him came flooding back. Her face warmed. Her body revved. Air became more difficult to breathe in. "He tripped over his bag."

"I'm fine, Ian." Dale straightened. "I should have slept more on the flight. I wasn't paying attention."

Ian's hot glare pinned Claire again. "Don't worry about it, Dad. It's a long flight and one that anyone would expect to be difficult for you."

Sophie looked from her son to Claire. "Ian, help your father down the rest of the steps. Claire, do you mind if I take your hand? My legs turned to JELL-O before I realized Dale can still land on his feet like a cat." She stepped past Dale.

"Absolutely." Claire met her on the steps and put an arm around her in support. "My heart did a summersault as well. Sorry if my hands are sweaty."

Once the four of them were on firm ground, Claire nodded for the driver to retrieve Dale's bag. He sprinted up the steps and did just that. Ian's accusation rang through Claire as they stood there. She blinked back tears as she imagined how much worse things could have gone.

It's my fault they're here.

If anything had happened to them, that would have been my fault as well.

What am I doing?

Dale straightened to his full height. "Claire, I'm fine, just not as graceful as I once was."

What could she say to that? She met Ian's gaze and returned his glare. *Does he think I don't already feel like shit? There's nothing he could say that I'm not already telling myself.*

Stand down, Captain Negative.

She looked Ian over and shook her head. *Why does my heart race every time he looks at me? What is it my body doesn't understand about him being wrong for me?*

Granted, the sex had been good.

It ranked as the best she'd ever had.

But this? The disgust in Ian's eyes? His heartless accusation and the fact that he was right?

That ranked as the worst a man had ever made her feel.

"Let's get you into a car, Dad. You'll feel better once you sit down."

As Claire watched Ian guide his father to one of the cars, she acknowledged what the lure of him was. Yes, he was a dangerous man. An angry one. But he was also protective of those he loved. Once the shock of seeing Ian passed, Claire admitted it would have been more surprising if he hadn't accompanied them. Or arranged for someone else to. His devotion to them was unlike anything Claire had experienced in her own life. A part of her craved a loyal partner like that. Someone she could lean on.

Not all the time.

Independence was important to her.

She had proven she was capable of surviving—of thriving—on her own.

But every once in a while . . . she wouldn't mind being able to curl up in the arms of a man who was strong enough to handle her tears. He didn't need to save her. Fix her. Just be there when she faced her demons and hold her.

She'd never trusted a man enough to let one in that deeply. Into her bed, yes. Into her heart, once or twice. But into the dark corners of her mind where questions remained and her confidence waned? No, she had yet to meet a man she thought could pull her back from the edge if she leaned out too far.

Ian was strong enough for sure.

Problem was he'd more likely shove her off the cliff than lead her back from it.

Be angry with me, Ian. I'm just as angry with you.

And angry with myself.

We shouldn't have had sex.

I take it back.

How great would it be if that option were possible?

Claire hovered while Ian settled his parents into the back seat of one of the SUVs. After he closed the door, he turned and demanded, "How far is the rental from here?"

"Fifteen minutes." Claire took a deep breath. "Everything is set up for them. My car is there so I'll be going with, but I can ride with the luggage while you go with your parents."

Ian opened the front door of the SUV his parents were sitting in. Rather than getting in as Claire expected, he gave the driver his phone number and instructed him to stay in constant sight of the other SUV. After closing the door, he said, "I'll ride with you."

Of course you will. "Okay, then, we're all set, I guess."

There was no hint of warmth in his eyes. "All set."

The driver held the door for Claire. She climbed in, moving all the way to the other side. Ian got in after her. Neither of them said a word until both cars had left the airport.

She braced herself for what she knew was coming.

She already knew what he thought of her.

What else could he say?

His face twisted before he turned to look out the window. Too late, she'd seen the pain in his eyes. He sat back and rubbed both hands over his face. "When I heard my mother cry out . . ." His voice was thick with emotion.

In that moment it felt as if the walls between them had fallen away. He wasn't Kade's angry, mysterious brother. He wasn't her wedding mistake. He was just a man who loved his parents and had suffered a scare. She laid a hand on his thigh. "I felt the same when I saw him stumble. I thought—I feared—" She took a calming breath. "But he caught himself. I'm sure he'll be sore. There is a hot tub at the house. We should encourage him to go into it for a few minutes tonight. I can also have a doctor come to check on him or we could stop for some ibuprofen or something. I believe that's on his approved list of over the counter medications."

His eyes riveted to hers and he flushed. "Stop." His gaze fell to her hand on his leg.

She pulled her hand back.

When his eyes met hers the walls were once again firmly in place. "We shouldn't have had sex."

"I agree . . ." she said lamely.

"If you think it gives you some kind of advantage, it doesn't."

"Advantage?"

"I'm not the type to be led around by my dick."

Normally even-tempered, Claire couldn't keep her cool around Ian. "That's so sweet of you to say. This is what I've missed the most about you . . . your soft side."

He turned so he was fully facing her, his broad shoulders blocking out the world behind him. "I don't know what game you're playing, but it's a dangerous one if it involves my family."

She turned also, unafraid and sick of defending herself to him. "I could say the same about you." When her words replayed in her head, she amended, "Except it's your family, so that doesn't make as much sense." She shook her head. "What I mean is I'm tired of your games as well. Don't act like I took advantage of you. It takes two to fuck."

"You've got quite a mouth on you."

"Because a man can say fuck but a woman can't? Fuck. Fuck. Fuck. Fuck you if you don't like me saying the word fuck."

A corner of his mouth twitched as if he'd almost smiled. "I didn't say I didn't like it."

There it was. The zing. The air in the car sizzled with it. Had they been alone Claire would have bolted because she knew what came next. *First I want to smack him, then I'm tearing my clothes off. Or not, because still dressed sex is apparently how I roll with him.* Anger was a much safer place so she returned to that. "Why are you here, anyway?"

His eyes hardened. "What do you want from my parents?"

Heat rose as Claire's temper did. "Is it so difficult to believe that I might simply like them? That they might like me?

That this might be about nothing more than us wanting to see each other?"

"Your business is tanking. Are you banking on them bringing in new clients? Your time might be better spent asking yourself why your clients left in the first place."

"It is not—" Her hands fisted at her sides. "You are so . . . so . . ."

"Right?" he asked in a smug tone.

She lost it. "You entitled, arrogant, asshole. First of all, I built up my business and my clientele on my own. No one helped me. I didn't have a trust fund to seed my success. I did it all on my own. And I'm more than capable of rebuilding without anyone's help. So I don't need your business advice, thank you. Second, I have no idea how someone like you came out of two of the nicest people I've ever met. Do you know how lucky you are to have not one—but two incredible parents? I lost my mother to drugs and my father . . . well, he could have been any one of her hookups. But you know what I'm not? I'm not bitter about it. And I'm not angry except when I hear someone like you . . . someone who was born with it all . . . sound like you think you're better than I am because you had everything handed to you. Who really understands how to make money? Those who started with nothing. Who values love the most? Those who have not had much of it in their lives. So, go ahead, judge me . . . question all my motives . . . your opinion of me doesn't matter because you don't. Not to me."

With that, she turned away from him. They drove along in tense silence. As she calmed, she couldn't help but add, "I did feel bad when your father almost fell. You may not want to see it, but I care about your parents, and I would have felt horrible if anything had happened to Dale."

IAN COULDN'T LOOK away from Claire's rigid back. Confusing as it was, he was fighting a nearly overwhelming desire to pull her into his arms and tell her he'd help her make everything that was wrong right again.

He didn't, though. Things used to be so clear to him. Right or wrong. Good or bad. Which was Claire? Which was he?

He wasn't used to going round and round with questions like that. Until recently, if a friend of the family had found themselves on hard times, Ian would have worked behind the scenes to bring new opportunities to them. Finding Kade had sent him into a tailspin and shaken his faith that he could protect the ones he loved.

He'd missed something so glaringly obvious he couldn't forgive himself for it. Was he now seeing guilt where there was none? He asked himself what he would have thought of Claire had he met her a year earlier.

I would have been impressed by her grit.

By her loyalty to Kade and Annie.

Would have been grateful for the way she cares for my parents.

Her honesty wouldn't sting quite as much as it does.

She's right.

I am an ass when it comes to her.

"Sorry." He muttered the word.

She glanced back at him. "Did you say something?"

How was it possible that she had become even more beautiful? His heart pounded in his chest. He didn't trust her. He didn't like who he was when he was with her, but there was no denying they had a connection. "No."

Her eyes raked his face. "Oh, because I thought I heard you apologize."

That was something else he liked about her—she was a ballbuster. He raised a fisted hand to his mouth and forced a cough. "Just clearing my throat."

"That's a shame because I would have accepted your apology." Her eyes flashed with challenge and his blood headed south.

Everything else fell away—unimportant in the face of the need raging through him. He wanted her—plain and simple. Sex the first time had been a mistake. Sex the second time . . . well, it just made sense to give it another shot. "I went back to your room the night of the wedding, but you were gone." He wasn't sure why he said it, but the words hung there in the charged air between them.

"I thought it was for the best," she murmured.

"Because you had someone waiting for you back here?"

"Because you're an asshole."

He barked out a laugh. She was a constant surprise. "Funny, that's not what you were saying when—"

She put a hand over his lips to stop him. "Don't even go there."

He kissed her fingers, then took her hand in his, returning it to his thigh, exactly where she'd laid it earlier. His cock was already pulsing for her touch, but it was neither the time nor the place to explore that. Their driver was slowing the car to open a gate to a private driveway. "What am I going to do with you, Claire Wendell?"

She met his gaze boldly. Time stopped. It became surprisingly difficult to breathe as he waited for her to answer. She pulled her hand back and her chin rose proudly. "Nothing. Been there. Done that. And it was a mistake." She wrinkled her nose. "Friends?"

Hell no.

"Sure," he said then leaned forward to whisper in her ear. "Friends still fuck, right?"

She shook her head, but her cheeks were a delightful pink; there was fire in her eyes, and she looked as if the comment had almost made her smile. For right then, while his parents were pulling up in an SUV behind them, that was enough.

Chapter Eight

LATER THAT EVENING, Claire stepped into her apartment and kicked off her shoes. *What a day.* She undid her skirt, stepping out of it and tossing it on the back of her couch. Normally a creature of habit and structure, she would have immediately placed her shoes in her closet and her skirt in the laundry.

She glanced around, yesterday's clothing was also hanging from the back of the couch. Her apartment was quickly becoming as messy as her life felt.

The Barrington visit was supposed to help her find her feet. She'd imagined a quiet tea or two with Sophie in which she would have shared just enough of her situation to get some motherly advice. Dale would have made some jokes that would have left her laughing. Their stay was supposed to help Claire feel better.

Instead Claire was a confused tangle of emotions and had spent the day pretending having Ian in the mix didn't change anything.

He changed everything.

As a rule, she didn't give in to her temper. Control was

the path to success. She stripped as she walked through her bedroom, tossing the rest of her clothing on her bed as she went.

It had felt good, though, to tell Ian exactly what she thought of him.

As she stood beneath the hot spray of the shower she asked herself some tough questions. *What am I doing? Am I sabotaging this life because I don't want it anymore? I'm so tired of being perfect, of showing others how to be the same.*

Is that the lure of Ian?

Because with him I feel gloriously out of control?

Isn't choosing that path the perfect way to lose everything I've attained?

She slid a long T-shirt over her head and padded to the pantry then stopped herself. *No. I need to make healthier choices.* So, instead she put on some soothing music and took out her yoga mat.

She considered putting workout clothes on then remembered reading an article about naked yoga. Many people came to yoga for the health benefits, but over time discovered that the core of it was much more spiritual. In meditation, in the calm of the stretches, acceptance for oneself could be found if a person sought it.

And naked yoga? It claimed to be the next step. When everything else was stripped away, when the exercise was raw and uninhibited, it was there the author of the article said a person could find a deeper peace within themselves.

She tossed her shirt across the room. It was worth a try.

The first challenge for Claire was to quiet the voice in

her head. She breathed in. She breathed out. She cleared her mind.

Her phone rang, and she cursed herself for not turning the ringer off. She considered ignoring it but decided it might be Sophie or Dale. Everyone else would have texted her. She scrambled across the floor and was slightly out of breath when she checked the caller ID.

Ian.

Ian?

Had something happened? "Hello?"

"I'm downstairs."

She nearly dropped her phone. "You can't come up."

"Why not?" His voice was deep and husky.

"I'm doing yoga." It was the best she could do. Her body warmed in anticipation of his touch and her thoughts scrambled.

"I do yoga."

He said it with such confidence she almost believed him. "Really? Why can't I picture that?"

"I had a Buddhist martial arts instructor who sold me on the benefits of it. I'll gladly prove my level of skill to you right now if you'd like. Show you some of my favorite positions."

She rolled her eyes at his blatant innuendo even as her body flushed. Sure, being with him again wasn't a good idea, but on the spectrum of mistakes . . . how bad was it really? She'd already been with him. It wasn't as if she were making a new mistake, involving another man. Like the three-second rule of dropped food. It fell in a gray area she was willing to defend.

Still, she didn't want to make it too easy for him. Clearly women had allowed his good looks to excuse his bad behavior. As a life coach, she'd guided other women through challenges in their relationships. She even had a cute analogy she started the session with. Many men were like puppies—they lived up or down to the expectations set for them. Allowed to do as they pleased, they'd leave shit all over your apartment and hump your friends. The good news? Many came around when they knew what their woman wanted.

This wasn't Boston.

Claire wasn't afraid Dylan and Connor might end up in jail.

This was her turf. If he wanted to play it would be by her rules. "You can come up, but only if you agree to my conditions."

"Sounds intriguing."

She rushed around picking up the clothing she'd discarded around her apartment. A few cups to the dishwasher and . . . presto, it was pristine again. "No touching until I ask you to and you don't stay the night." Clear expectations. Clear boundaries. That's what she advocated with her clients and she'd seen it work for them time and time again.

"I'm stepping into the elevator."

Claire frowned and her reaction confused her. The old her, the life coach who was perfectly happy remaining single and saw nothing wrong with sex for the sake of sex, was at direct odds with the new Claire who had recently realized she might want more.

Ian isn't Mr. Forever.

He's not even my next week.

At the knock she opened the door with a proud tilt to her head. The warm air from the hall danced over her bare skin. His eyes widened and a grin spread across his face. Her chin rose as she met his eyes with confidence. She closed the door after he walked through it.

I'm doing him. She let out a shaky breath. *On my terms.*

He stepped closer.

She stepped back.

"I'll get you a yoga mat," Claire said.

He placed a hand on the wall by her side, blocking her retreat. "I like your style." He leaned closer, so close his breath tickled her parted lips.

She swallowed hard and tried to remember why she didn't want to start with sex. "Only touch when I ask," she reminded him huskily. "But you should probably strip. This is naked yoga."

His eyes never left hers, but he dipped just a little closer until the heat of his body warmed hers just a hair shy of making actual contact. "That's a new one to me. So, does that make you my instructor?"

Oh, he was good—at being bad.

"I guess that depends if you're man enough to take instruction." *Bam. What do you have to say to that?*

"Oh, I'm man enough." The hot promise in his eyes was sexy as hell.

"We'll see, won't we?" she asked. Rather than feeling bad about where this was headed, Claire decided to consider him nothing more than one last slice of chocolate cake before cutting sugar out of her diet again. Some mistakes were worth making—once, twice . . . She licked her bottom lip as she imagined a third time as well. He'd be gone in a couple days and then her search for a real relationship could commence. *But for tonight . . .* "First, I need to get your mat."

He stepped back and lowered his arm. She slipped away to the closet where she was certain she'd put her extra mat. As if this were something she'd done before, she placed it in front of hers in the middle of her living room floor. All the experience she had to pull from was an article she'd read about couples' yoga poses. She'd passed the article along to one of her clients who had been searching for ways to deepen her intimacy with her husband. Her client hadn't shared details, but she'd claimed to have been pleased with the results.

Time to pretend I know what I'm doing. Claire sat on one of the mats and said, "Sit behind me. Back to back."

"One minute," Ian said. Claire's heart missed a beat when she saw that he was folding his clothing into a neat pile on the couch. It was nearly as beautiful a sight as his perfectly sculpted naked ass and deliciously muscled back. *He's a neat freak. Swoon.*

As he walked toward her, his large bouncing erect cock drew her attention. *Oh, yes.* She blushed and raised her eyes to his. "Ready?"

"Evidently," he said with humor that also shone from his eyes. Wait, did he have a sense of humor? Where had that been hiding? "Back to back. Okay." He settled into a seated position on the mat behind her, leaving an inch between them.

Claire turned then leaned back against him. Bare skin to bare skin. Almost innocent. So erotic. She took a deep breath.

He did the same.

Slowly their breathing synched. In and out. Deep calm breaths. Claire closed her eyes and tried to clear her thoughts. Rather than the peace she normally found, her senses were overwhelmed by the scent and feel of the man behind her . . . in the most amazing way.

She opened her eyes and attempted to speak, but her first attempt came out a little strangled so she tried again. "Now turn your shoulder to the right and place your hand on my left knee while I try to do the same."

They each twisted slowly, deeply, until they could reach the knee of the other. It had them facing in opposite directions, but each breath he took felt like one she shared. She'd never felt so connected to a man.

That he wasn't mocking or rushing the experience surprised her. After twisting the other way, they did seated side bends.

"What now?" he asked in a husky tone.

"We could try a shared boat pose."

"Is that your norm?"

We don't have much but we should at least have honesty. "I've never done this before, but from what I've read it's good for building intimacy."

His breathing deepened. "You wouldn't say we've already

been quite intimate?"

Seated as they were, it was easier to be honest. "Sex and intimacy are two different things. Before you, I didn't think I was capable of enjoying sex with someone I don't like."

"Before you, I didn't know I could enjoy sex with someone who never shuts up."

She inhaled sharply before responding. "Are you rude to me because you think it's funny or because you don't realize when you sound like a complete ass?"

She expected another off the cuff comment. Perhaps a joke. "The women I date usually say I'm charming."

"Really? Anyone say that recently?" Her intention wasn't to sound as snarky as she did. She was genuinely curious.

"I've been a bit too preoccupied to date lately."

Interesting.

"Preoccupied with business or family?"

He sighed. "Do you really want to talk about this now?"

"We don't have to. We can just have sex. I'll probably still enjoy it. But sex without intimacy is like cake without frosting. Or frosting without the cake. Yes, that would be a better description. It's a sudden jolt of indulgence, but not nearly as satisfying."

They sat in silence for a moment. Their breathing slowed until it once again found a common rhythm. "I'm not big on desserts, but if what you're saying is that we should like each other before we fuck again—it's not a bad goal. So, show me this boat pose of yours."

Wow, well, at least he's being honest as well.

Claire shifted forward a few feet then turned. He was

already facing her, fully excited, but looking as if he actually did want to try the next pose. "So, I guess we link our hands."

She held both hands out and shivered when his strong ones closed around hers. Their eyes met and she almost caved. It would be so easy to let go and let nature take its course. The memory of his kiss was still so vivid. She remembered exactly how good being taken by him felt. However, she also remembered his comment he'd uttered during sex. Like she could have been anyone. *Because that's what happens when you have sex with someone you don't like. You get some of how you feel right back at you.*

And even if you tell yourself it doesn't sting—it does.

We could have that again.

Or maybe, just maybe, we could have something more.

They sat there, legs bent, hands clasped on either side of their knees. She moved her feet forward. He did the same. As fluidly as if they'd done it a hundred times before they pushed upward so their feet rose between them. His legs were longer but they adjusted their distance until it worked. With her view of his face obstructed by her own shins, she said, "I didn't like when you said you knew I'd be a good fuck when we had sex. It made me feel like I didn't matter at all to you."

His hands tightened on hers. "That was wrong of me to say. I apologize. I was lashing out at you about things that weren't your fault." They lowered their feet and met eyes over their knees. "I don't like that you think you know what's wrong with me when you hardly know me."

They pushed forward, their feet rising again, blocking their view of each other once more. With soothing music in the background and them working together as they were, his words didn't put Claire on the defensive. This was simply two people lowering their walls and letting the other person in. "I'll try not to do that anymore, but it's hard for me to sit back and watch you not appreciate what you have."

"Fair enough," he said as they lowered their legs. Taking the lead, he moved his feet outward, taking her feet with his—spreading her legs wide. She was wet and ready for him. He was aroused to the point that likely wasn't comfortable. He leaned back, bringing her forward until her face hovered near, but not quite able to reach his cock.

She pulled back, leaning back until he was the one bent before her, and said, "I want to be in a relationship, but not with someone like you."

As he pulled back, his eyes held hers. "I don't want to be in a relationship, but if I did it would be with someone like you."

As their bodies adjusted to the stretch, her legs widened farther. Some might have felt exposed and vulnerable, but she felt powerful and deeply connected to the man across from her. "That's the nicest thing you've ever said to me."

"It's the truth. My family adores you. You've proven to be a loyal friend to Annie and Kade. Even if you are trying to benefit from linking your name to ours, I'm not sure I care anymore. It doesn't appear to be hurting anyone."

Her hands tightened on his and her teeth ground together. "Let me see if I understand what you're saying. You're fine with me *using* your family because they seem to be okay with it?"

He was wise enough to not agree. "I could have said that better."

She yanked him forward. "Or not at all."

He slowly pulled her up until they were face-to-face in the middle. "No man in this position could be judged for not articulating his thoughts correctly. Very little of my blood is circulating up to my brain."

She almost smiled at that, but didn't allow herself to. "I'd let it slide if it wasn't on par with how you always sound."

"Sadly, the inability to think straight is a condition you bring on frequently." Still holding her hands, he shifted himself into a kneeling position. There was over a foot between them, but the air between them was pulsing and his excitement was waving eagerly up at her.

She did the same. "Is that another compliment?"

His smile returned. "Do you like those?"

"Every woman does. When they're sincere." She couldn't resist, she let go of one of his hands and reached down to stroke his cock. He moaned with pleasure.

"Holy fuck," he growled. "How about I choose the next position?"

A shudder of pleasure shook her. "Which one do you suggest?"

"The supine back arch," he said as he ran his hands down her arms. "Lie back."

She went onto her back and brought her feet beneath her so she could lift her hips off the mat and moved her arms over her head.

"Wider," he commanded.

She inched her legs apart.

"Perfect," he murmured. "So fucking beautiful." He didn't ask permission, nor did Claire complain, when he moved between her legs and began to kiss his way up her thighs. He didn't dive right in. Instead he took his time. His hands caressed her legs. His mouth worshiped her inch by inch.

Those fingers of his—those amazingly knowledgeable digits. If he were her Mr. Forever she'd want to know where he'd learned to do . . . *ah, yes . . . that . . . and that.*

Maybe I wouldn't want to know.

I'd feel like I should send a thank you card and . . . "Oh, God, don't stop."

I LOVE NAKED yoga.

There wasn't too much Ian felt comfortable endorsing with such conviction, but he could have spent all night in this particular pose. He loved the taste of her, the sounds she made each time he did something that drove her wild, and when she finally came, he loved how she cried out his name with a fair amount of profanity.

In public, Claire was polished. He'd watched her hold her own at events full of movie stars, the ultra-wealthy, as well as royalty. Only in private did one see that she had another side to her—a grittier one.

She wasn't the first woman he'd been with who had been comfortable with nudity, but she was the first who was so *real* and expected him to be as well. *Imagine how good sex will be between us once she actually likes me.*

He rose to his feet, bent, helped her to hers, then kissed that beautifully dazed smile of hers. Her hands were everywhere on him. His hands followed a similar greedy path over her body. With his tongue he teased and circled, plundered and claimed, until he was shaking with the need to have her.

In a move that took even him by surprise, he swung her up in his arms. "What are you doing?" she asked as she caught her breath.

He strode across the living room and down the hall to the open door of her bedroom. "It's called the He-Man toss."

When he came to a stop beside her bed, she laughed and clung to his shoulders. "Don't you dare throw me."

He soaked in the beauty of her, bare chest heaving, huge smile, laughter shining in her eyes. A moment like that does funny things to a man. For just a second Ian could picture waking up with her in his bed, not just tomorrow, but always. He shook his head to clear it and tossed her then stood there, making a show of scratching his chin and looking around. "Now, where would someone like you keep duct tape?"

She was up on her feet with admirable speed. "No way in hell are you tying me up."

"Not even just—" He motioned toward his mouth. He wasn't serious, but he was enjoying the reaction he was getting from her too much to stop.

She threw a pillow at his head, but he ducked just in time, and it sailed above him. "I bet you keep it right beside your bed." He opened the drawer, not expecting to see anything, but whooped when he saw both a vibrator and condoms. "You like to be prepared. I respect that."

Distracted by his glee, he didn't see the next pillow she swung at him until it connected with his face.

"How about respecting someone's privacy?" Her words were harsh, but she was laughing, hands on her hips, so damn proud of herself he just stood there, dumb with desire for her.

He turned to face her fully. "Did you just hit me?" he growled while fighting back a smile.

She wrinkled her nose at him. "To be fair, you were looking through my things."

"Still, can't let you think there isn't a consequence to something like that." In a move his martial arts instructor would have been proud of, he grabbed one of her ankles and swept her feet out from beneath her. She hit the mattress for the second time. "I have a reputation to uphold."

He crawled up onto the bed beside her, taking both of her hands and holding them above her head in one hand. A feat that was only achievable because she let him, but it was still a powerfully exciting move. He ran his free hand along her jaw, down her neck, across her breasts and slowly down to cup her sex.

"The one where you're charming?" she asked breathlessly.

He dipped a finger between her folds and loved that she was still wet and ready for him. Still, he preferred her mindlessly begging for him. "I'm also known as a formidable opponent."

"Are we on opposite sides?" She gasped as he began to work her clit with his thumb as he moved his other two fingers in and out of her.

"I hope not." His tone was more serious than he meant it to be because he'd answered her honestly. He didn't like the confusion he saw enter her eyes so he kissed her, until he felt the tension leave her.

I don't want to fuck her.

I don't want to be frosting to her.

He rolled onto his back and pulled her into his arms, simply holding her until their breathing synched as it had when they were on the mat. He kissed her forehead and sorted through the mess his head was in. "I understand why you don't like me, Claire. I don't like myself much lately. If it was as easy as deciding not to be angry, I would."

She melted against him. "I know how that feels, Ian. I have my own demons, and sometimes they win."

"I should leave." Despite believing those words, he didn't move. "I don't want you to regret being with me."

She raised her eyes to his again. Her expression was so tender, so supportive. "See, when you're like this, I could almost like you."

A smile tugged at the corner of his mouth. "Almost?"

The light in her eyes told him she was having fun with him this time. "Do you know what would clinch it?"

He ran a hand through her hair. "What?"

She tapped a finger on his chest playfully. "A night of really, really good—I mean mind-blowing, multiple-orgasm sex."

He laughed and rolled her beneath him. "Oh, is that all?"

"It would be a start."

The smile they shared was one he would always remember. It was in that moment that he realized he might have found a woman he would never want to say goodbye to.

Then he did his best to give her everything she'd asked for . . . that night . . . and again in the morning.

Chapter Nine

WARM AND WITH a smile on her face, Claire slowly awoke. The arms around her pulled her closer, and she heard the steady beat of a heart within the muscled chest she was using as a pillow.

Wait.

What?

Her eyes flew open and she groaned. *I said he wouldn't spend the night. It was one of the conditions I set right up front.* She searched his face. Would he feel equally uncomfortable when he woke to find himself still in her bed?

Probably not.

Even asleep there was an undeniable confidence to him. He was a physically fit, successful man in his prime. Too damn good-looking for his own good. No wonder he had such a healthy ego—Claire didn't know a man who could compare to him . . . in or out of bed.

She'd called him arrogant, but the term was an attempt to pigeonhole him. In reality, every time she thought she had him figured out, he surprised her. No, he couldn't be dismissed as simply arrogant.

He was a powerful man. What he used that power for, she didn't know, but she doubted many men dared to clash with him. And not because he was rich. Even the press danced to his tune. So many of her clients would kill for his level of confidence. Money didn't buy that.

Nor did being good-looking.

People either had his kind of swagger or they didn't.

She smiled as she imagined him as the lead man in a James Bond movie. Espionage. High-tech weapons. Behind-the-scenes government toppling. That was her fantasy version of him. No one spoke about how he'd made his money, outside of that he received a modest trust fund just like his siblings. They'd grown that nest egg in different ways. Asher was known as a shark in the business world. Grant was an investment guru . . . and was credited for strategically growing the overall wealth of the Barringtons. Lance was an architect, Kenzi a public speaker, both rich more or less because of how well Grant had managed their trust funds.

But Ian?

He was the mystery man. Like Asher and Grant he was considered at the top tier of wealth globally, but no one spoke of why.

A difficult man to get to know.

Complex.

Unexpected.

In more than one way.

She traced the line of his pecs as she remembered another way he'd surprised her the night before. That the sex had been good? No, she'd expected that. What she wouldn't have predicted was how open he'd been with her. How willing he'd been to allow her to take the lead. He listened. Gasp, he apologized.

Ian.

Ian had not only said he was sorry but had also shown her he was vulnerable to her criticism. "I don't like that you think you know what's wrong with me when you hardly know me."

Not defensive—honest in a raw, real kind of way.

I can't believe I told him I want to be in a relationship but not with him.

Or what he'd responded with. "I don't want to be in a relationship, but if I did it would be with someone like you." Although it did sound like a version of "It's not you, it's me . . ." it had still rung true to Claire.

And better than if he said he didn't like me either.

Although he did say he never thought he could enjoy sex with someone who never shuts up.

Oh, yes, and that he is okay with me using his parents because they don't seem to mind.

I'll circle back to both of those in the future.

Which shouldn't come as a surprise to him, since according to him I never shut up.

A memory of how he'd woken her with a kiss a couple of hours earlier for a "bed slamming against the wall" romp brought a smile to her lips. *I wasn't talking then.*

Afterward, basking in the afterglow of several orgasms, she'd fallen asleep without the need for uttering a single word. *See, if he wants me to be quiet, he just needs to keep me in that fully sated state.*

Keep me? A thought came to her that wiped the smile from her face. *That sounds like this will happen again, and it can't. This isn't the beginning of us, it's closure for something we shouldn't have done in the first place.*

At least we've come to a place where we aren't angry with each other anymore. That'll help when we see each other again, because we will. While he's here with his parents and then later when I visit Annie and Kade.

His eyes opened and he ran his hand up and down Claire's bare back. "Morning."

She forced a smile. "Morning."

He brought a hand to the side of her face and combed his fingers through her hair. "What has you looking so serious?"

She took a moment to consider how she should answer. This wasn't the first time she'd woken with a man in her bed. She wasn't a shrinking virgin, but she hadn't found herself in this particular situation before. He wasn't someone she could lead to the door and never see again. Nor was he looking for more than this from her.

For this not to be a problem, she had to make herself okay with all of it. They had to put the brakes on this now, before she felt more invested in something that had nowhere to go. "Nothing, just going over my schedule for the day. I arranged for the Martins to fly in today to visit your parents. Harrison would have come but he has to tend the bar. Your parents seemed to really get on with Annie's parents, so it should be a nice visit. I was planning to join them, but since you're here I could head into the office instead and make some calls."

Ian frowned. "My parents are here to see you."

"I'm not going anywhere. I'm sure they'll want to have dinner together tonight. The chef I lined up for them is top notch. His dishes are not only delicious, they're also healthy. I know how important that is for Sophie and Dale, and he is aware that the less of a deal he makes about the modified ingredients of his recipes the more Dale will enjoy them."

"Claire."

"Let me say something first, Ian." She rose up on her elbow. She didn't want to hear what he was about to say. Morning-after conversations were often ripe with false statements said simply to ease the awkwardness. That was fine when it involved someone she wouldn't see again, but this was Ian—the new brother-in-law of her best friend. If they did this wrong, they might walk away from their time together even more uncomfortable than they'd been before. Time to adult. "I don't regret last night. Annie is like a sister—the only family I've ever really had. She's important to me. Your whole family is. You and I are finally in a good place. You'd say that, right?"

"A good place. Yes." He rolled up onto an elbow as well, his face so close to hers she nearly forgot what her point was and kissed him.

She didn't. Morning was the time for sanity to return. "We can move forward now. We had our issues, but we talked them through. Obviously, there was a sexual attraction between us, but we've resolved that as well."

"Resolved," he echoed the word as if testing it out.

All hint of the laughing, lighthearted Ian was gone, but Claire pushed on. "We're both mature adults. We know not everything leads somewhere. The important thing is we've gotten to a place where we can be in the same room without any tension."

"That's the important thing."

She smiled tentatively. "And I can finally say I like you."

His frown deepened, but he didn't say anything. When he raised a hand to caress the side of her face, she ducked away from it and skirted out of the bed. She could have covered herself then, but she wasn't ashamed of what they'd shared nor was she embarrassed by the human body. "So, I'm going to take a shower—alone. It would probably be best for both of us if you head back to your parents."

His expression was closed, unreadable.

Part of her wished he'd protested a little. She was doing what was right, but did it have to look so easy for him to go along with? Whatever. She walked to the bathroom door then turned. He hadn't moved. "I'm only a text away if they need anything. I can't imagine you would, but please don't tell your parents you were here last night."

"Is that all?" he asked in a cold tone that surprised her. She was giving him the Hail Mary of next-morning escapes. He'd said he didn't want a relationship. They'd had great sex. She'd even experimented with her oral sex technique until she got it just right with him. What was he possibly unhappy about now?

Hesitating at the door of the bathroom, she chewed her bottom lip. Was he worried that his performance had been subpar? Some men were like that. "It was all great, though. Easily the best sex I've had in a long time."

"Go shower, Claire." He rolled to a seated position, dropping his feet to the floor. "I'll be gone before you finish."

Still she hovered. This wasn't the reaction she'd expected. A smooth parting kiss. Some slightly offensive dismissive comment he said without thinking—yes. Moody, broody Ian? He wasn't supposed to return. "We're good . . . right?"

"We're good." He stood.

Her gaze dipped to his cock. Unlike the night before, it wasn't engorged and waving eagerly at her. Still impressive in size, but disappointingly uninterested.

Which is for the best.

This is where we need to be.

"See you tonight at dinner, Ian." She stepped into the bathroom and closed the door behind her, slumping against it. Through the door she heard his footsteps as he made his way out of her bedroom. She waited, not moving, and heard the water in the hallway bathroom turn on then off. A few minutes later, the door of her apartment slammed shut.

Slammed.

She straightened off the door. Could she have handled waking up next to him better? Maybe.

She'd been afraid if she didn't lay out a plan for them to succeed, things would end up awkward between the two of them. Would that happen when she saw him at dinner?

She turned on the shower and met her eyes in the mirror while waiting for the water to warm. Her face was pink and there was a general well-loved look about her. She'd find this again with a man who she had something in common with.

Or she'd remain single.

Either way, Ian was now off-limits. That was the only path that made sense.

A CAR WAS waiting for Ian by the time he was on the street. As expected, the driver had remained in the area all night. Nothing less would have been tolerated.

As he slid into the back seat, he gave the man's face a closer look than he normally would. He looked tired. Had probably slept in the car to be close. *God, I am an entitled prick.*

He decided then and there to make sure the driver was generously compensated. No, he wouldn't lower his standards, but he could make sure a sleepless night or two proved worth it to the man. So much of what Claire had said to him was swirling around his head.

He didn't like that he'd left without saying much at all to her, but he was all tangled up on the inside. Yes, he'd told her he wasn't looking for a relationship. Yes, he'd meant it. No, he hadn't liked hearing her say that whatever was between them had been "resolved."

What the fuck was that?

Thanks for the great sex . . . don't let the door hit you in the ass on your way out.

And it had been great.

The best she'd had in a long time? Not the best she'd had period. She was either lying or he was in way over his head. Sex with Claire was in an entirely different league than what he'd had with other women. Not that it hadn't been good with them, because it had.

So, if you're wondering, Claire, yes, I've had fantastic sex with other women.

What was different with Claire, though, was how he *felt*.

Above the waist.

She challenged him.

Made him laugh . . . as well as see things in a new way. Before, he would have never thought sitting back to back with a woman could feel as intimate as anything they'd done sexually. For the first time in his life, he'd felt a real connection to a woman.

Like they'd shared every breath.

Like they'd been two halves of a whole.

And that feeling and the sex that followed had changed something in him. He didn't want to just have sex again, he wanted to come down from an orgasm feeling a little shattered—with her. Being with her moved him to a level he was struggling to explain.

When she looked at all uncertain, he wanted to slay her demons.

When she smiled, he wanted to be the reason.

And the thought of her with another man was enough to have his hands clenching at his sides.

Never had he thought he could feel this . . . territorial.

The irony? She'd made it clear the night had not been special to her. Maybe she fucked every man with that same enthusiasm.

As the driver pulled onto the road where his parents were staying, he conceded that he wasn't angry with Claire—he was angry with himself. He was being an idiot.

This was about his pride—nothing more.

I should call her and thank her for handling this morning as gracefully as she did. Now we are free to both go on with our lives, guilt free.

After thanking the driver, he slipped into the house. He was showered and changed before he sought out his parents. They were seated in a sunroom with Mitch and Hazel Martin, Annie's parents. As he entered the room, his father and Mitch got to their feet.

"Finally," Dale said. "We were afraid you'd sleep the day away."

"G' day, mate," Mitch said before greeting Ian with a hearty handshake. He was an older, studious-looking man, a perfect match for his earthier wife. The two owned a beer brewery and ran a pub. They had easy-going, everyone-is-always-welcomed personalities that complemented both businesses.

"Good to see you again, Mitch." Ian walked over to greet his wife with a light kiss to the cheek. "Hazel. More beautiful every time I see you."

She blushed. "Ian, say that again so my husband buys me flowers this week. It's never good to let a man get too comfortable."

Mitch returned to sitting beside her. "I don't need anyone to remind me how lucky I am to have you." He kissed the side of her head before adding, "You tell me all the time."

"Oh, you." She elbowed him, but she was smiling. "For that you get to match the socks this week. I'm on sock strike."

He put a hand to his heart. "Anything but that." Then he looked around with a pained smile. "She's serious. And if I don't match them just right I'll never hear the end of it."

A general laugh followed.

His mother added, "I don't know why no one has invented self-matching socks. Ian, have one of your techie friends look into that. I'd like a pair for Christmas."

"Sure," Ian joked. "I'll get right on that."

"And I'd buy them." Hazel snapped her fingers. "No wonder you Barringtons do so well. If I could shake a basket of socks and have them all seek out their partner on their own, I'd never wear a regular sock again."

Mitch put his arm around her. "Then how would you torture me?"

Her smile widened. "I'm sure I'd think of something."

Ian took a seat and propped his feet up. Seeing his parents smiling and laughing with Annie's family was improving his mood. Kade had chosen well, both with his wife and with the people he'd considered his extended family. Mitch and Hazel had been the first people Kade had turned to when he'd learned he was a Barrington. These were the people his brother trusted the most, outside of Pamela and Dave, who had raised Kade as their own.

No wonder Kade was so fucking happy. No he hadn't been raised with money, but his life had been full of this.

Ian's family had only recently become a place where he and his siblings could be themselves. For too long, there had been a forced perfection when they gathered. Always tense. Always struggling to maintain the illusion that nothing was wrong.

His parents were barely recognizable as the people they'd been back then. Dale was openly more loving, infinitely more patient with his children, and happier than Ian ever remembered seeing him. Sophie was more vibrant, more outspoken, and stronger than any of them had imagined. Together they looked like a couple who'd been given a second chance at love and were embracing every moment of it.

"Too bad Claire isn't here. We were looking forward to seeing her," Hazel said.

Sophie poured a glass of water from a tray beside her. "Stay for dinner and you will. She said she had a few hours of work but would be by later. I get the feeling things aren't going well for her. She was such a help when Kade and Annie came to Boston. I hate to think that being away for so long might have affected her business adversely."

"Is that what she's saying the problem is?" Ian asked. He was genuinely curious. If time away was the reason, he regretted the comment he'd made to her about losing her clients.

"She's not saying anything," Dale answered. "It's technically none of our business, but we care about her. If she's having a hard time, we'd love to help out any way she'd allow us to."

"I'm so glad you said that, because we heard something . . ." Hazel exchanged a look with her husband then stopped.

Mitch shook his head.

"What did you hear?" Dale asked.

Mitch leaned forward, clasping his hands between his knees. "It's nothing. We didn't actually hear it, Harrison did."

Hazel waved a hand in the air. "He's always had a sweet spot for Claire. He's a little young for her, but the older they get, the less that matters. I'd love to see the two of them end up together."

No way in hell that would ever happen. Harrison was a nice enough man, but soft—goofy. He wouldn't know what to do with a woman like Claire.

Sophie clapped her hands together. "Your son is such a sweetheart. If they married, Claire would join our family via yours. Any chance we could lure him to Boston to open a pub there?"

With a growl, Ian said, "What did Harrison hear about Claire?" Dale shot Ian a look meant to silence him, but Ian needed to know. "Or her business."

Hazel hesitated then gave her husband's arm a pat. "They won't be offended. It sounds like a misunderstanding."

Now Ian really was curious.

Mitch cleared his throat. "We heard through the grapevine that Claire has lost most of her clients. It started soon after you found Kade, but the mass exodus happened while she was in Boston. Since she wasn't around to look into it herself, Harrison headed down to Melbourne and met with a couple of her ex-clients. He came back with the impression they were concerned that associating with her was something your family wouldn't approve of. Harrison said someone had spoken to them, asked a bunch of questions about their business dealings with Claire. To them, it felt like a criminal investigation. They were concerned about being associated with her if it was. Harrison said one person who'd spoken to them was American and connected to your family. I don't know why they thought that, only that they did."

In a rush, Hazel added, "No one is saying you sent anyone to speak to her clients. We're only hoping that seeing you here with her will end the rumors that your family was questioning her character."

Fuck. Did Bradford spook her clients? He was supposed to be discreet. *Shit.*

With full confidence, Dale said, "I can assure you whoever was asking about Claire is in no way associated with our family, but we will absolutely make it well-known that she is above reproach in our opinion."

Ian braced his hands on his thighs. "This may be my fault."

Dale frowned and directed his first comment to Mitch. "Ian takes time to warm up to new people. He sees everyone as guilty until they prove their innocence."

"Because often they are guilty," Ian ground out. "Isn't Kade evidence enough that blindly believing anyone without looking into them first is a recipe for disaster? If we had—"

"Enough, Ian," Dale's voice was suddenly hoarse. "I am fully aware of the role I played in—"

"Ian Alessandro Barrington—tell me you did not send someone to harass Claire's clients," Sophie's tone was unusually sharp.

Ian sat up straighter, his tie suddenly tight around his neck. "Harass—no. Ask some clarifying questions—yes." He winced at the look his parents exchanged before turning back to face him.

Dale shook his head in silent judgement. Growing up, Asher had been on the receiving end of that look many times, but it was a new experience for Ian, and he didn't like how it made him feel. His father had always been his moral compass. Loyalty to wife and family, even when it cost him his career. Faith in humanity. These were the things Dale lived rather than preached. His parents didn't just say they wanted to help those less fortunate, they poured time and resources into charities and organizations that over time had made a real difference in the lives of many.

His father was a good man. Not a perfect one, not a strong enough one to keep their family safe, but someone Ian admired. Dale's disapproval brought back to mind Grant's warning that Ian might not be on the right side anymore.

Sophie wagged a finger at him. "Well, now we know what you'll be doing with your time. None of us are leaving until you've made this right."

Mitch and Hazel looked painfully uncomfortable. He said, "We shouldn't have said anything."

Sophie's eyes didn't leave Ian's face as she responded to Mitch. "No, we're grateful you did. This is unacceptable, Ian. You haven't been yourself since we found Kade, but it's time for you to move on. Focusing on the past is bringing out a dark side of you, and this is proof of it." She stood and walked over to where Ian was sitting. "What happened was horrible, but don't carry the weight of a guilt that belongs on my shoulders. I'm the one who held Kade. Your father didn't see him alive. I did. I knew he didn't die at birth—knew it, and I let the doctors convince me I had imagined it."

When her voice cracked, Ian rose to his feet and pulled his mother to him for a hug that he needed as much as she seemed to. "It wasn't your fault, Mom. None of this was your fault."

She cupped his face in her hands. "Nor was it yours. Or your father's. My sister wanted to hurt our family and she succeeded. Sometimes I think if she were still alive I might put aside my belief that violence is never the answer and wring her neck. But I can't because she's gone. There is no one left to punish. And that's frustrating as hell, isn't it? I get it. All those years our family was in pain . . . someone should pay for it. But if my sister were suddenly in this room, alive and well, and I had a chance to hurt her . . . I don't know that I would. I don't want to become her." She stepped out of his embrace and wiped a tear from her cheek. "And I can't bear the idea that a child of mine is on that path. She was a bitter, paranoid woman who couldn't love anyone because she couldn't let go of the past. Yes, she was hurt, but she nurtured that wound, and in the end it tainted every relationship she had. The kind of anger you have, the need you feel to even the score, if that takes root in your heart . . . I'm afraid I'll lose you too. And she will have won. Do you see that, Ian? She's still hurting our family, but this time she's using you as a weapon. Don't let her win. Don't let her take us down twice."

Ian swayed on his feet and blinked a few times quickly. His family swept things under the rug. They denied—they pretended. He didn't know how to respond to such a raw display of emotion from his mother.

He looked around. Mitch and Hazel were no longer in the room.

His father took his place beside his mother. "Listen to your mother, Ian. I wish I'd been smart enough to hear her a long time ago."

Sophie put an arm around Dale. He bent to kiss her forehead. "We are more than what happens to us. Don't give anyone the power to change who you are, Ian."

Ian raised his gaze to meet his father's. "I had no idea looking into Claire's company had caused issues for her."

"But now you do," Dale said gently.

"Now I do." He took a moment to face the emotions crashing over him. Anger with himself for being the source of more pain for his parents. Regret that he was likely the reason Claire's clients had pulled away. Shame that he'd let his desire for vengeance lead him down a path that had his parents worried for him—the protector of the family.

Although his parents were not happy with him for having an extensive background check done on Claire, that wasn't all this was about. To them, it was a sign that he'd lost perspective.

And he had.

He was in too deep.

His parents weren't just asking him to repair Claire's client list. This conversation had unspoken layers to it. They were looking for assurance that he would honor his role in the family.

If the fixer found out something ugly about Pamela, he wouldn't destroy her.

Because that would destroy Kade.

And in turn whatever peace our family has found.

I would have to live with that and the knowledge that I was the one who handed Aunt Patrice yet another win.

After a strained silence, Dale said, "I should go hunt down Mitch and Hazel before they leave more than this room. Are we good?"

His mother searched his face.

Ian nodded. "We're good." When neither of his parents moved, he added, "Claire's phone will soon be ringing with returning clients."

A smile returned to his parents' faces. "That's my Ian," Sophie said softly. Just when he thought the conversation was about to take a good turn, she added, "You slept out last night. I didn't realize you knew anyone in the area."

Ian's face warmed.

Dale clapped a hand on Ian's back. "Sophie, I'm sure we

don't want to know. When it's someone important, he'll bring her around. Right, Ian?"

"Absolutely," Ian answered, forcing a smile.

Dale's hand settled on Ian's shoulder, and he gave it a healthy squeeze. "Unless he was with Claire, but Ian's too smart to choose someone so close to the family. His intentions would have to be serious for that not to be an issue."

He knows. Ian met his father's gaze, but it wasn't easy. He couldn't lie to Dale so he said nothing.

Sophie laughed. "What a disaster that would be. I know I'm the one who had hoped for a match, but the more I think about it the happier I am nothing developed. Kade is so laid back, but I wouldn't want to see his reaction if he thought you were messing with his wife's best friend. Ian, whoever you were with last night, I love her already for being the reason we dodged that bullet."

Ian nodded then caught movement outside. "Mitch and Hazel are heading toward their car. I'll go tell them there's no reason to leave. Then I have a few phone calls to make. Set a place for me at dinner, though."

"Will do," Dale said.

With that, Ian strode out of the room then sprinted to the driveway to catch Annie's parents. Even as he smoothly apologized and encouraged them to come back inside, his thoughts kept returning to his father's not so subtle warning about Claire.

As a rule, Ian didn't date anyone closely associated with his family.

He'd certainly never been with any of his brothers'

friends, not even friends of friends.

With Claire, all rules went right out the window.

His.

Hers.

The real pisser?

He was looking forward to dinner with his parents and the Martins because she would be there. Deny it as much as he tried to, he wanted to see her again.

First, though, he had a wrong to right. As he planned how he would do it, his mood improved. He was a man of action, and if there was one thing he knew how to do well, it was convince people his way was the right way.

The only safe course.

After locating the office in the house, he closed the door and sat down at the leather swivel chair behind the desk. Leaning back, he propped his feet up on the corner of the desk and opened Claire's file on his phone. He had a list of every one of her former clients.

Without hesitation, he called the first. Chad Nerwick. Son of an Australian investment banker, daytime television personality. Others might have been fielded by Chad's manager, but the only numbers Ian had in the file were direct ones.

Chad picked up on the fourth ring. "Chad, Ian Barrington."

There was a long pause. "How did you get this number?"

"It has recently come to my attention that the actions of one of my employees might have been misconstrued. I believe Bradford was the one who contacted you."

"Am I in trouble? If this is about the drugs he found, they belonged to my friend. I don't do that shit. I'm clean."

Interesting.

Sad too. Like shooting fish in a barrel. "Bradford can be . . . how can I say this nicely . . . intense. If he looked into your personal life to the point where he would have uncovered anything questionable, that means you refused to speak with him."

"Damn right I did. Dark glasses. Suit. Scars. Scary fucking dude. Demanded to speak to me. I didn't know if he was with the government or the mafia. Dude, he threatened to expose my manager's affair if he didn't set up a meeting with me. That's some fucked-up shit. No way was I getting involved in that. Then he comes to the studio with my—with my friend's cocaine and wants to know about people I work with."

"He came on too strong. I'll talk to him about that. My fault, I pulled him from an assignment in the Middle East for this. I forgot how serious he takes his job." Ian cleared his throat. "He asked you about people you work with—people like Claire Wendell."

"Yeah. A lot of questions about her. Dude, I barely know her. My father thought I needed someone to help me with my image. Whatever she is into, I don't know anything about it. I swear."

"She's not into anything. In fact, that's the reason for my call. I'd like you to hire her back. Nothing different. Just have her do whatever she was doing for you before."

"I don't want to do that."

"I believe you do."

"I really don't. Like I said, I'm clean now. So even if you have someone search my apartment, they won't find anything. I'm done with drugs."

"Do you know who I am, Chad?"

There was another long pause. "I did ask my father about you."

"How old are you?"

"Twenty-five."

"Twenty-five. That's definitely old enough to know the difference between a good offer and a bad one."

"I guess so."

"What I'm offering you is a chance to wipe the slate clean. Together we can turn back the clock, fix what shouldn't have been a problem. Were you happy with what Miss Wendell was doing for you?"

"Yeah. I mean, she created a workout schedule I still follow. I've used her suggestions when I did a few interviews. Is that what you're talking about?"

"That's what I'm talking about. You should give her another chance."

"And if I don't?"

Ian let his silence be his answer.

Chad's voice rose. "Are you threatening me?"

"I don't make threats. I do, however, remove them. You're not a threat to me or Claire, are you, Chad?"

"I'm not afraid of you. I'm recording this conversation. What do you think of that?"

"No, you're not. Go ahead, take a minute. See if you

were able to record any part of this conversation. I'll wait. You can even call me back if you need more time."

"Shit. It didn't record. Why not? Are you doing something to my phone? Can you do that?"

Ian sighed. "I don't have time to list everything I'm capable of. Let's get back to the matter at hand, shall we? Claire is a wonderful woman who was clearly a good influence on you. You should give her a call today and ask her if she has space in her schedule for you."

"I don't know if that's a good idea."

"I'd consider it a personal favor if you did. Something I'd remember."

"And if I don't call her?"

"I'd remember that too."

Another long pause. "All I'd be agreeing to is to work with her again. Nothing more than before."

"Nothing more. It would be as if Bradford had never been by to see you."

"Okay."

"Okay," Ian repeated, then ended the call.

He opened Claire's file again and pulled up her next client. Sloan Byder, professional golfer. *I wonder what Bradford found on him.*

Chapter Ten

THAT EVENING CLAIRE pulled into the driveway of Sophie and Dale's rental home, but didn't immediately get out of her car. She liked to joke that after years of dealing with clients from all walks of life, not too much surprised her anymore.

Nothing in her experience, however, had prepared her for the day she'd had. The craziness of it had started with a call from Chad Nerwick himself—not his manager—requesting to work with her again. She'd felt euphoric—hopeful that his call was a sign that, given time to reflect upon what she'd done for them, her clients would return. She'd still been flying high from speaking to Chad when another former client, Sloan Byder, had called and also requested to once again work with her.

Those two calls alone would have carried her happily through the rest of the day, but when her phone had rung again with yet another former client wanting her back, it began to feel like an orchestrated event. Sprinkled between prior clients, there were calls from prominent Australians requesting more information about how she might help them.

As soon as one call ended, another came in.

There was only one explanation for her afternoon: even though she had yet to speak to Sophie and Dale about what she was struggling with at her company, they must have somehow found out. That wouldn't have been difficult, considering that some of her former clients had been vocal about breaking off their association with Claire.

It was impossible to feel good about the resurgence of business, though, because it made Claire feel like she was doing what Ian had accused her of. *I've never been that person.*

I'd rather not have clients than have Sophie and Dale believe that's why they're here.

And Ian—all this does is support everything he already thinks about me.

Claire jumped at the knock on her car window.

Ian.

She lowered the window because she had a feeling her legs would be shaky if she got out right then. She forced a smile.

Ian didn't smile back.

Why would he? We only get along when we're having sex.

Or naked.

Her face flushed as she remembered just how wonderful things could be between them. *Sadly, dinner with his parents does not allow for either.*

She pictured Sophie's shocked expression if she ever even joked about that in front of her and coughed back a nervous laugh. As she met Ian's gaze, she told herself it wasn't her fault that her thoughts went haywire around him. All it took was a look from him, exactly the kind he was doing right then, to set her heart pounding and her body warming.

Apparently my vagina didn't get the memo that we're done with him.

"Coming in?" Ian asked.

She let out a shaky breath. *He is not the only man on the planet who will ever make me feel this way. Don't be stupid.* "Of course. Just lost in thoughts about work."

"Good day?"

Did he know what his parents had done? If so, his expression gave nothing away.

"Unusual for sure." She pushed the door open and stepped out. As she straightened, her arm brushed against his chest and it was electric.

Totally normal and it will pass.

He stepped closer. So close she fought the urge to throw her arms around his neck and greet him the way her body craved to.

He searched her face almost tenderly. "I've said some things I shouldn't have—judged you unfairly. This has been a harder year for me than I am comfortable admitting. I want you to know that I finally see that."

Is this some kind of joke?

Is he playing with me? Trying to get me to admit something?

He looks sincere.

"Thank you," she croaked.

"Let's start over." He held out his hand. "Hello."

She hesitated then placed her hand in his. "Hello."

"You look amazing tonight," he said without releasing her hand.

Fireworks went off inside her. Full brain meltdown. "You do too."

He smiled and she found herself smiling back.

"For our first date I thought we should start with something different. What do you think about dinner with two old married couples?"

He was joking of course, but she tensed and clarified, "We agreed to move forward as friends."

His smile widened. "I don't remember agreeing to any such thing."

She tugged her hand free. "You did. This morning."

"Oh, you mean when you said whatever is between us is resolved."

"Yes."

"The problem is, it's not resolved for me. Being with you again is just about the only thing I thought about today."

Whoosh, there went Claire's ability to think again. That day she'd fought a similar affliction, but she'd made peace with the reality that it couldn't happen again. "We shouldn't do this."

He ran a hand through her hair. "We shouldn't do more meaningless, mindless fucking. I agree."

Ouch. He sure doesn't hold back.

"But what if this has the potential of being more? What if what I'm looking for from you is more serious in nature?"

"You said you weren't looking for more."

"You've never changed your mind?"

Claire shook her head. "Relationships don't work that way." She hugged her arms to her waist. "I'm not even sure you like me."

"Do you require more proof?" His smile slanted to a grin.

The heat in his gaze was enough to support his claim. Okay, so he valued honesty. "I'm not sure I like you."

"That's not what you said this morning."

She sputtered in surprise at his comeback until she saw a hint of laughter in his eyes. "This isn't a game to me."

He leaned in. "Do you think it is to me?"

Breathe. Keep your head. "I don't know you well enough to say what this is."

"That's an easy fix, wouldn't you say? I just asked you on a date. The next move is yours."

She hedged. "I was already going to dinner with your parents."

He took a moment before answering, "I'm interested in you. Interested enough to conceal every touch, to sneak every kiss, to hide this for as long as we can—but I'd rather walk inside holding your hand. I'd rather look my parents in the eye and answer honestly when my family asks if there is something between us."

Was this conversation really happening?

Was Ian actually saying he wanted to date her openly?

Would his tune change once he heard what his parents had done for her?

If they went public, it would be much harder to simply

end it. Things would always be potentially awkward. It was a risk she wasn't sure she was ready to take. "Right now no one knows about us. If we tell your family and you *change your mind* again, it'll be complicated."

"So careful. Another thing I like about you."

"Another? Is it a long list?" She held her breath—waiting—needing to know.

Placing his hands on her hips he pulled her against him. She moved her hands to rest on his chest. "Extensive and growing. You're intelligent, beautiful, caring. I like how you challenge me, make me laugh, make me think."

"Even how much I talk?"

His eyes lit with desire. "I'm exploring techniques of dealing with that."

She chuckled. "Techniques, huh?"

"So far, they appear to be mutually satisfying." He kissed her then and every reason she had for why this was a bad idea faded away. This was where she wanted to be, and kissing him felt like coming home.

When he raised his head, they were both breathing heavily, and she was even more confused. The idea of walking into dinner simply holding Ian's hand was as tempting as it was intimidating.

I just told myself this was over.

If we end this now, we both leave with memories of good sex and with our hearts intact.

Ian says he wants more.

What if he means it?

What if he doesn't?

When I headed off to Melbourne, people told me I'd never make it.

They laughed at the idea of me coaching the already successful.

I proved them all wrong because I believed in myself.

The only way this could work is if I believe in Ian.

Once I do—I'm all in.

She searched his face. "I want more than meaningless, mindless fucking too. I never thought I'd say this, but my career is no longer enough for me. I'm looking for someone I can add to the world's overpopulation problem with, a real partner, someone solid enough to help me believe in forever. I'm not sure it's possible, if I'm capable of that kind of love, but that's what I'm looking for."

"Then I'm your best bet. I doubt another man could handle you." He laughed when her mouth rounded with surprise. "And I haven't met another woman who could handle me. That alone means this is worth a shot."

"Worth a shot." She repeated his words, testing them out. "You're quite the romantic, aren't you?"

He hugged her closer. "I'm a lot. I get it. If you don't think you have what it takes to bring me to heal, I'll understand."

She saw right through him. "Just how easy do you think I am to manipulate?"

"Not easy at all, that's another thing I like about you."

Okay, he's saying all the right things.

Still, she couldn't agree to anything until she'd told him about her day. His reaction would be all the answer she needed. If it made him doubt her again, she was done. If he believed she was just as surprised as she claimed to be—she was ready to take a leap of faith with him. "Before we go inside, there's something I need to tell you—"

"Ian? Claire?" Dale called from the doorway.

Oh, crap. Claire jumped out of Ian's arms, but it was too late. Dale was standing in the doorway with a disapproving look on his face.

"Coming, Dad," Ian said. He held out his hand for Claire to take.

She wasn't ready to make the leap. She wasn't ready to close the door to the possibility of him either. Could she trust him?

Could she love him?

If she didn't give this a chance, would she spend the rest of her life regretting not being brave enough to find out?

IAN SAW THE indecision in her eyes and respected her more for it. He'd had the afternoon to debate the merit of moving forward with her, she'd had about five minutes.

Still, it felt like an eternity passed as he stood there waiting to see if she would take his hand. He would have preferred the decision been made without the added pressure of his father watching them, but life rarely worked out according to plan. Ian's long-term success had been in part due to his ability to change direction and adapt.

And that's what he'd done earlier that day.

He'd heard everything his parents had said, had digested it, and in the end concluded they were correct. There were two paths before him . . . one that kept his goals and his priorities in line with his family's and another that did the exact opposite. Was the truth worth the devastation that might follow its reveal?

All too easily he could remember years of wishing he had the power to turn back the clock and save his family from the hurt that had followed the loss of Kade. Did he really want to be responsible for ripping him away from them a second time?

His mother's pleas had echoed in his head many times that day. Aunt Patrice shouldn't have the power to weaponize him against his family. She couldn't be given that win.

Even if it meant never knowing the true reason Pamela had escaped to Australia with Kade. Shudder, Asher might just be right. Her motivation didn't matter as long as the result was as good as it appeared.

Kade claimed to have had an idyllic childhood.

His parents had their child back, granted called by another name and after years of mourning him, but there was no denying how much happiness Kade's return had brought them.

It was time to let the past go.

And Claire?

No woman had ever claimed that much space in his head.

He'd said he didn't like who he was with her, and he'd meant it at the time. Between making calls that day, he'd replayed their time together. Winced as he remembered all the stupid shit that had come out of his mouth. Smiled when he remembered how beautiful she'd looked as she'd told him off each time.

She wasn't afraid of him.

She didn't back down.

Didn't run from a fight.

Not many women could handle the complexity of the life he'd built for himself. On one hand it required a surface polish. On a regular basis he mingled with the world's most powerful people. Any woman he chose would need to be able to do the same. Claire could. There were times when his lifestyle attracted unwanted attention and even danger. To survive as his partner, a woman would have to be able to navigate those waters as well. She'd have to know what she could share, what had to be concealed, and when bodyguards were a necessity rather than a luxury.

Claire was the first woman he could imagine handling all that.

And him.

She had all that strength, and somehow still took the time to make sure a chef knew how to get his father to eat healthier. She was a good friend, a good businesswoman, and would most likely make some man a phenomenal wife.

Wife.

Is that where this is going?

Should I even be starting something with her if I don't know?

All I'm sure of is that I'm not ready for this to end.

And waiting for her to decide if she is willing to give us a chance is damn near killing me.

Their eyes met and held.

He wished he could declare something that would sway her, but neither were in that place yet. He'd been honest about it. She'd been honest about her own feelings.

Come on, Claire. Let's do this.

She breathed out audibly and took his hand in hers as a huge smile spread across his face. Their fingers laced, and he bent to kiss her lips briefly.

Together, they walked up the steps to where his father was still standing. It was a tense moment, but Ian was determined it wouldn't remain that way. "Dad, you know Claire, my date for dinner."

"Your date?" Dale looked from Ian to Claire and back. "We talked about this."

Claire's eyes widened. Ian brought her hand up to his lips and gave it a quick kiss. "We did, and I heard you."

"Are you sure you want to do this? Your mother—"

"Will be happy when she sees that we are," Ian broke in. "Dad, nothing comes with a guarantee, but I want to do this right." He glanced down at Claire.

She nodded and gave his hand a squeeze.

"Okay," Dale said then cleared his throat. "I just hope the two of you know what you're doing. Come on in; Mitch said he was hungry an hour ago—but Hazel convinced him to wait. Let's get some food in that man before he passes out."

Ian laughed. "That's Dad's way of saying he's hungry too."

"Maybe," Dale said smoothly, closing the door behind

Claire and Ian after they walked through it. "And prepare yourselves—Sophie is going to be pretty surprised. She didn't see this one coming."

"But you did?" Claire asked.

"Yes. As soon as Ian chose to ride to the house with you instead of us, I knew there was something between the two of you." Dale stopped and in a low voice said, "Be kind to each other—no matter where this goes. That's all I ask."

Ian's eyes riveted to Claire's again. *Kind.* No, he hadn't always been that with her. "Is that the secret to making it work?"

Without missing a beat, his father replied, "It's the secret to being able to look yourself in the mirror and not hate the person looking back. Relationships aren't easy. Even at their best, they're messy, gut-wrenching, all-consuming. Nothing will ever cut as deeply as a look of disappointment in the eyes of the person you love."

"Wow, you're not selling this well, Dad."

His father continued, "But nothing beats that feeling when you get it right. The memory of the day she vows to be yours forever. Or the first time you hold a baby the two of you made together and laugh and cry at the same time because it's so damn scary but you're trying to look like you're ready for it. It's just you and your partner after that, doing the best you can, trusting each other, picking each other up each time you stumble."

"Stop, Dale, you're making me cry," Claire said with a tearful laugh.

My father sure has changed. It fit, though, with the changes he'd witnessed in Dale since his youngest sister, Kenzi, had confessed she'd been raped but had hidden the truth from her family out of shame. She'd been the first to crack the veneer of their picture-perfect family.

Dale was no longer restrained, seemingly always in control. Perhaps his recent health scares also contributed to his apparent change of heart when it came to the appropriateness of displaying one's real emotions. The return of Kade certainly had contributed too. The father who'd raised Ian and his siblings would never have entered into this conversation. He wouldn't have wanted to know, and he certainly wouldn't have allowed anything that might upset his wife come to the dinner table.

Ian had always loved his father. Theirs was a complex relationship. Love wasn't blind. This new, stronger version of his father was late in coming but refreshing to see. Through hell and back, Dale and Sophie had stuck it out and come out the other side just as much in love as they'd ever been. Ian saw that clearly now.

His whole family was undergoing a metamorphosis. One by one, his siblings fell in love and married. Happier now than they'd ever been alone.

It was a powerful enough change to get Ian thinking.

Still, that didn't mean Ian was ready to talk marriage and babies. "Dad, let's start with a dinner."

Claire chuckled and wiped her eyes. "Yes, please."

When his father turned and continued walking, Ian mouthed, "He means well," and started walking behind him with Claire.

"I know," she whispered back.

As soon as they entered the living room, Sophie rushed over and gave Claire a bone-crushing hug. "Look at the two of you. I don't know why I ever doubted Alessandro. I couldn't wait and called him about you, Claire, but he told me to hang tight because he already saw something in the works for you. How does he always know?" She turned and hugged Ian just as tightly. "You'd better be good to her."

"I'll do my best, Mom."

She wagged a finger at him. "You'll do better than that. This is Claire." Then she smiled. "What am I worried about? You're here with her. You wouldn't do that if you weren't serious."

I might not have thought this entirely through.

"I didn't want to hide what we're doing," he said.

"What are you doing?" His mother's eyes rounded. "How long has this been going on?"

Claire stepped in smoothly. "It's all very new. So new, we don't know how it will work or if it will." She raised their linked hands. "But we hope you'll be patient with us as we see where this takes us."

Hazel joined them. "Claire has always had such a good head on her shoulders, hasn't she? It's refreshing to see. So many people jump in without thinking things through. That's never been her."

"Oh, sometimes I jump," Claire said with a blush as she met Ian's gaze. He hid a smile.

I love that I'm the exception to her rules. It'll be fun seeing just how many of them she'll bend for me.

Oh, yeah.

As if she could read his thoughts, she gave his side a light smack and under her breath said, "Stop."

He put an arm around her waist and murmured in her ear, "Only for you."

Her eyes sparkled.

His heart thudded wildly in his chest.

In the background, Mitch said, "They do make a nice couple."

Dale added, "That they do. Let's move this party into the dining room. I hear the chef has planned a culinary delight. Thank you for finding him, Claire. You have impeccable taste."

The look he gave Ian was easy enough to interpret—*Don't disappoint us.*

Chapter Eleven

IT STILL FELT a bit surreal to be seated next to Ian, laughing with him over stories his parents shared about him as a child. Her mood swung back and forth between hopeful and afraid it would suddenly end.

She hated the insecurities that had surfaced in her recently. Normally, she was confident.

Even when her company took a hit, her doubts had been fleeting. In her heart she knew the success of her present company, or whatever she decided to do next, was within her control.

Love was not.

Family was not something she'd always wanted. The truth was painful to admit.

Annie's parents had been in the background for most of her life, but she'd kept an emotional distance from them for the same reason the Barringtons scared her. Never having something was hard. Almost having something then losing it would be torture.

Sophie and Dale said she was already like family to them. *Like family* wasn't family. *Like family* didn't involve unconditional love.

Does unconditional love really exist?

I'd like to think I could feel that for any child I had.

If my mother felt it for me, she didn't show it.

She pushed food absently around her plate. *I'm not my mother.*

I refuse to be.

She raised her eyes from her plate and planted a big smile back on her face. *Annie found love. Sophie and Hazel did as well. There is no reason why the same couldn't happen to me.*

"Are you okay?" Ian whispered in her ear.

Claire blinked a few times quickly. "Yes. Just too excited to eat, I guess."

"How was your day at work, Claire?" Sophie asked from across the table.

Her question took Claire by surprise. How could she have forgotten? She almost didn't say anything, but maybe it was better to talk it out with everyone involved. If Ian chose not to believe her, well, his parents would see that too. It would make her decision not to move forward with him understandable. "Sophie. Dale. I am so grateful to you for your friendship and your support. I guess you know that my company recently lost a significant number of clients."

"We do," Dale said gently.

"Everyone hits a rough patch now and then," Sophie added.

Mitch and Hazel murmured their support, but they looked almost . . . guilty? Claire dismissed the idea and said, "Today my phone did not stop ringing. Everyone who'd left suddenly decided to come back. I know you did that for me." Tears filled her eyes. "I just wanted to say that I never expected that level of support from you, and I don't know how to thank you enough. I was having a bit of a pity party for myself a few days ago. I shouldn't have shared that with you, but it felt so good to have someone to talk to." She sniffed. "I don't know what to say other than thank you and please know that you don't have to do anything more for me. I'm already grateful to be in your lives, and I can take care of myself."

Claire turned to gauge Ian's reaction. He didn't look surprised. Or angry. Was he happy that his parents had stepped in to help her?

"Claire"—Dale called her attention back to him—"I wish Sophie and I could take credit for your windfall of luck, but we didn't do anything."

"You didn't?" Claire shook her head. It had to be them. Or could it be their mere appearance in Melbourne had been public support enough?

Hazel clapped her hands together. "I wonder if Harrison had something to do with it. I wouldn't be surprised if he called all of your clients individually to ask them to take you back. He's always been a little sweet on you." She stopped when she appeared to remember Ian. "Nothing ever came of it, of course. And he'll be happy for the two of you once he hears that you're together. If it doesn't work out, though—"

"Oh, for God's sake, it was me," Ian growled.

The table fell silent and all eyes turned to him. He threw his hands up in the air. "I was the reason you lost your clients in the first place. It made sense that I should be the one to convince them to work with you again."

Another long silence.

Claire opened her mouth to speak, closed it, then tried again. "How were you the reason I lost my clients?"

Mitch stood. "Look at the time. Hazel if we don't leave now, we'll be flying back in the dark."

"Right. It was wonderful to see you all." Hazel stood as well. "Really, we'll have to do this again soon."

Dale rose to his feet. "Sophie, why don't we walk them to their car."

Sophie joined him, but she hesitated at the doorway. "I hate to leave them to talk this out on their own. What if he doesn't explain himself well?"

Dale chuckled. "Ian is a smart boy. He'll figure it out." With his arm around Sophie he led her out the door.

She ducked her head back in long enough to say, "Use your heart, not your head, Ian. Speak from your heart."

Alone with Ian, Claire laid her hands on either side of her plate and braced herself. She needed a moment to gather her thoughts. When Ian touched her back, she shrugged his hand off. "I'm going to ask you a couple of questions, and I need you to be honest with me."

"I've never been anything but," Ian replied as he turned to face her, resting his arm on the back of her chair.

Claire stayed as she was, facing forward. With him so close, if she shifted, she might lose herself in the loose circle of his arms. She might find herself wanting to run her hands up those parted, muscular thighs and forget to ask the questions that needed to be voiced. "How were you responsible for me losing clients?" She kept her gaze on her still full plate of food. "And was it deliberate?"

"Look at me, Claire."

"No. Tell me first. I can handle the truth. Your family doesn't need to know. Yes, it will change things between us, but I'd rather put my energy into rebuilding than rehashing how it happened. You made it right. We're good. Even Annie will never know. Just tell me the truth."

She barely took a breath in the pause before he spoke. If her mother had taught her anything, it was that people disappointed even those closest to them, but regardless of the pain it brought, those disappointments were survivable. *I wouldn't be who I am today if I'd had a mother who coddled and catered to me.*

I'm stronger because I had to learn to do for myself.

No matter what Ian says, it won't change who I am or how much I care about his family.

"It wasn't deliberate, but I understand why you'd have to ask." His voice was tight. "You didn't meet me at my best. I'm not making excuses for my behavior. I've always prided myself on doing the right thing, even when it was the hardest path before me. I saw my father have his political career ripped away from him, watched my family endure the shame of that scandal. The media said he used taxpayers' money to support his mistress. I learned early that it was lie. He was too good of a man to defend himself, to defend us. I swore then that no one would ever hurt my family again." He let out a harsh breath. "Then Grant found Kade, and I realized that when it came to what had hurt my family the most—I had done pathetically little. I had the resources to uncover the truth, but I'd never looked for him. I have to live with that."

Claire turned her head and met Ian's gaze. She was well acquainted with Kade's reintegration back into the Barrington family. She'd had a front row seat to most of Kade's life in Australia as well as to the aftermath of the news that he wasn't who he thought he was. She had a real sympathy for how his reappearance had affected everyone involved—even Ian. What was new, though, was to hear Ian share how it had made him feel. She could tell him that nothing that had happened had been his fault, but Asher had said as much to him. He hadn't believed it then. He wouldn't believe it from her now. Instead she focused on his reason for bringing that into the conversation. "You're afraid to miss something else."

He shook his head, then a pained expression twisted his face. "Yes." He raised a hand as if to caress her face, then dropped it before making contact. "Everyone associated with Kade's abduction is either dead or innocent. How convenient is that? No one left to punish."

"If you found someone to punish, after you did whatever you'd do to them, what would be different?"

His hand fisted on the table. "I'd know I'd done something."

Her heart ached for him. "I don't know if that would be enough. The last time I spoke to my mother I told her I wouldn't give her any more money because I knew it was only going to drugs. She overdosed a few days later. The man who sold her drugs went to prison for armed robbery and died in a fight there. None of what happened to him made me feel any better. What if I could have been the one to arrange his death? Would that have brought me comfort? I don't believe so. Partying and drugs were more important to my mother than I was. She died alone. Some might say she got what she deserved. My grandmother didn't want me and made that clear. I wasn't there when she died, and I didn't go home for her funeral. I don't feel good about any of it. Am I a horrible person? I don't want to think so. Could you have found your brother had you looked? Maybe. I don't have all the answers; no one does. All I can do is keep trying to be the best version of myself."

He nodded. "My mother said just about the same thing about her sister and what she'd do if she were still alive. I heard her here." He pointed to his head. "But when you say it, I hear it here." He laid a hand on his chest.

She lowered her eyes as a flash of doubt came and went then met his gaze again. "I want to believe you. I am a survivor and a fighter. I'm also strict about what I let into my mind and body because that's all I can control."

He ran a hand through her hair. "I could say the same about myself. I could also add that I'm unable to sit back and do nothing when I see an injustice."

"You don't have to be angry to make a difference. I don't allow myself to be. I deserve to be happy. You do too."

He pursed his lips. "You lost your clients because I had an extensive background check done on you. I didn't realize that the scrutiny might affect your business. I should have, but I didn't make that connection until earlier today."

She touched his arm. "Did you really contact all of my old clients?"

"I did."

"What did you say?"

"I suggested they give you a second chance."

"That's it?"

"Pretty much."

Turning fully toward him, she cocked an eyebrow. "So, one call from the great Ian Barrington was enough to have them all clamoring to work with me again?"

He flexed his shoulders and a grin spread across his face. "Impressive, isn't it?"

She studied his expression. He was making a joke out of something that in reality bordered on unbelievable. Yes, the Barrington name carried weight in Australia, but not even her highest profile clients had the kind of clout he was dismissing with a smile.

Just having money didn't give someone that level of persuasive power. "What aren't you telling me?"

His expression turned more serious. "Ask me anything."

There were so many things she didn't know. She started with what mattered most to her in that moment. "Do you still believe I would use your family for financial gain?"

Without hesitation he said, "No."

The tension that had been pulsing through her melted away. "Good. Because I couldn't be with someone who saw me that way."

He laced one hand with hers. "Then it's a good thing

we're starting over. I didn't trust you before this trip."

As long as they were being so honest . . . "I wasn't sure I could trust you either." She wiggled her fingers between his. "Even tonight. I thought your parents were the ones who'd called my clients. I was certain you wouldn't handle that well."

"We have a long way to go, don't we?"

They did, but their differences no longer felt insurmountable to Claire. "I have a hard time trusting people."

"We're fucked," he joked.

She chuckled. "I'm serious."

"So am I. I've never been good at relationships, but I value honesty. If you do too, no matter where this goes, it won't be a total disaster."

There was a vulnerability in his admission and in his round-about request for her to remain real with him. It was a moment she didn't want to end. This was a man she could be herself with—see herself with.

She'd shown him her darker side . . . and he hadn't so much as flinched. He was the first man she'd told about how her mother had died, the first person she'd told that her grandmother didn't want her. The latter was an ugly truth she hadn't even laid at Annie's door. Part of her had always feared that saying it out loud would give the memory power in the present. It didn't, though. It hadn't made her feel less worthy of being treated well. And Ian had accepted what she'd said in a way that made her glad she'd shared it. She'd invited him in, shown him a part of herself she didn't like, and it hadn't changed the way he was looking at her.

If she needed him to, Ian could hold her while she cried and not think her weaker for leaning on him. Like her, he was both a survivor and a fighter. They had more in common than she'd ever imagined.

They were starting over in a very good place.

"Is it safe to come back in?" Sophie asked from the door of the dining room.

"It is," Claire and Ian said in unison, both smiling as they realized they'd answered that way.

"I told you they'd be fine," Dale said as he and Sophie took their seats at the table again. "Ian is too smart to let a woman like Claire get away."

After taking a sip of her wine, Sophie pinned Ian with a look. "So, what stage would you say the two of you are at? Will we be scheduling more trips to Melbourne or planning a wedding?"

"Sophie." Dale gave her hand a pat. "There's no need to rush them."

"I'm only asking because if Claire is picking up a full client load, it sounds like she plans on staying here. Of course, Ian is free to live where he wants, but I had hoped . . ."

Oh, boy. It was way too early to have this discussion—but Sophie's concern was real. While living with her and Dale, Claire had seen how important it was to Sophie that her children were close to her. They gathered for game nights and family dinners. Nothing mattered more than family to her, and it was so beautiful Claire blinked back tears in the face of that kind of love.

Sophie was the glue that bound the Barringtons together,

and the reason Kade had decided to spend more than half of each year in Boston. Of course Sophie wouldn't want Ian to move to Melbourne.

Claire didn't owe any of them an explanation, but now that the walls were down she wanted to keep them that way. "I don't actually know what I want to do with my business. It used to be my top priority, but it didn't leave room in my life for anything else, and I've recently decided I want more."

"More," Sophie said with a happy sigh. "Did you hear that, Dale? Ian, if her definition of more is giving me grandchildren and moving to Boston, you are marrying her this weekend."

Ian choked on a sip of water.

Claire began to think she might have been too honest.

Dale laughed. "Stop, Sophie, before you spook them right into breaking up."

Ian's head snapped toward Claire. "Wait a minute, your phone rang all day with clients asking to work with you again and you're not sure you even want to be an accountability coach anymore?" He frowned. "I made all those calls for nothing?"

He looked like a boy who'd gone to the trouble of washing the dishes only to discover they were disposable and going to hit the trash anyway. "To be fair, I didn't ask you to call anyone."

His frown deepened.

Even sulking, he was adorable. Poor Ian. What he'd done really was incredible. "Making those calls was the nicest thing anyone has ever done for me."

"You're just saying that to make me feel better," he growled.

"Is it working?" she asked then wiggled her eyebrows at him.

Slowly a smile returned to his face. "A little."

Sophie broke in again. "I have the perfect solution."

Please don't suggest marriage again.

"Sophie—" Dale started.

"I spoke to Dylan and Connor. Clay introduced them to a producer friend of his who thinks they're star material for the big screen. Grant's looking over the contract. This is a big opportunity for those boys. They could use someone on their side, helping them navigate this project, especially if it leads to more."

Dylan and Connor? Claire gulped down some of her wine as she tossed Sophie's idea around. She had experience with helping people in the film industry. Success wasn't simply about on-screen presence, it was also about becoming a brand . . . building a social media platform . . . staying in the public eye in a way that grew one's popularity.

Ian ran a hand through his hair. "The meatheads are the perfect solution?"

Claire gave his thigh a light slap in reprimand. "You're only allowed to use that nickname if you do so with affection. They're really kind of sweet once you get to know them."

"Sweet." Ian circled a hand around one of his wrists as if flashing back to having them bound. "Not quite the way I'd describe them."

"It would take you to New York, Claire," Dale interjected. "Arguably the ideal place for you to discover what you'd like to do next."

And to the city Ian does most of his business from.

A helicopter ride to Boston—for those game nights and dinners.

"I've been considering making some changes, but relocating to the States would mean truly starting over." *For a man. I swore I would never be one of those women who dropped everything to follow one.* "I'd need a work visa. . ."

She looked into Ian's eyes, trying to read his thoughts on the matter. If he considered holding hands in front of his parents a big step, the idea of having her in New York must have him shaking in his shoes.

No denying it would add pressure to what they were doing.

Say something, Ian.

"I'm sure we could arrange for whatever you need." He looked around the table then met her gaze again. "It's a big move, though."

She swallowed hard. "Too big?"

"That depends on where we think this is going."

She nodded without speaking.

He rubbed a hand over his chin. "I don't want you to give up your life here for—"

There it was . . . exactly what her decision relied on. *For—*

He doesn't know if we'll make it, either.

He wasn't saying he loved her. He wasn't promising her

forever. Another woman might have seen that as a bad thing, but he was so refreshingly honest. Claire kissed him then, a brief, gratitude-filled smooch that ended with them both smiling. "The only way New York makes sense is if I'd want to be there with or without you."

"I agree," he said, his eyes lighting with a warmth Claire read as approval.

"I'll make some calls. Look into the financial feasibility of relocating."

"Factor in that you have two potential clients already. Depending on how you structure your schedule and rates, you could have a lucrative business that leaves time for . . . *life*."

A life with him?

Claire remembered they had an audience and blushed when she saw Sophie's expression. She was clutching Dale's arm and could not have looked happier with what she was hearing. Dale was smiling as well.

"It's definitely worth looking into," Claire said, suddenly breathless.

Sophie rested her head on Dale's shoulder. "I like them together."

Dale kissed her hair. "Me too."

Me three.

Claire turned back toward Ian. "What are your plans for tomorrow?"

He couldn't say the first idea she saw in his eyes, but it did widen his smile. "I don't know. What *are* my plans?"

"Would you like to see my office? Learn about what I

actually do?"

Dale sat forward. "I'd be interested. We've heard so much about it."

Sophie laughed. "Dale, this is the part where we give them time to sort it out on their own. On that note, I have a book I'm looking forward to diving into. Come on, Dale. Our work here is done."

Ian rose to give Sophie a kiss and Dale a hug.

Claire did the same.

A moment later, Claire cleared her throat and said, "So, I should get home." Her cheeks warmed, but she held his gaze. "You're welcome to stay over if you want."

His answer was a long, deep kiss that took them to the brink of shedding their clothing right there. When he raised his head, he was flushed and his eyes were burning with the same hot desire that licked through her. "I'll get my bag."

IAN MADE LOVE to Claire slowly that night, tenderly. This time it was different, from the first kiss in the dining room back at the rental to the way she'd fallen asleep draped over his chest and was currently snoring softly.

He shifted so she settled more comfortably against his side and savored the feel of her in his arms. She belonged there—in his bed—although technically they were in hers. Either way, it felt right. More right than anything had in a long time.

If she decided to move to New York, he would need to make changes in his own professional life to keep her safe. Before her, had someone asked him if he would rein in his international endeavors for anyone, he would have said, "Hell, no."

He wouldn't be giving it up just for her, though.

Not if he were honest with himself.

He'd fought the fights he'd thought were worth potentially dying for, and he'd done it all with the bravado of a man who had nothing to lose. Funny, he hadn't realized until then that he'd begun to think of himself as expendable.

Nothing, not even the peace that came after a sex marathon with Claire, could change Ian at his core. He'd never be able to sit back and not get involved, but he might no longer have to do it from the front line. He didn't have to choose anger.

He would make a difference in ways that wouldn't endanger Claire and the children they'd have together.

Holy shit, I can see myself having a family with this woman.

He smiled down at a still sleeping Claire. Part of him wanted to wake her up and tell her that he'd just imagined a future with her and it had looked pretty damn good.

She moaned and rolled over in his arms, using one as a pillow and his side as an ass rest. *Beautiful. Blissfully quiet.*

He chuckled.

If she knew what I was thinking she'd make me pay for that one, my little fighter.

His mood sobered as he remembered how she'd sounded when she'd talked about her mother and grandmother. He'd known the facts of both deaths. Bradford was thorough when it came to background checks. His latest report had even included the balance of Claire's savings account. She'd saved enough to be able to relocate to New York without his help, but she wouldn't have to.

What hadn't been in Bradford's report was how devastating it must have been for Claire to have been left with a grandmother who didn't want her. Although she'd spoken of both of their deaths calmly, he couldn't imagine either had been any less devastating.

What had she said about who appreciates love the most? Those who have never known it? Even on the worst day he'd had as a child, he'd been secure in the knowledge that both of his parents loved him. It gutted him that she hadn't had the same.

He rolled onto his side and wrapped himself around her. If it was within his power, she would never know that feeling again.

Chapter Twelve

CLAIRE STOOD IN the living room of a fully furnished Upper Manhattan condo and hugged her arms around her stomach. For a woman who'd always found comfort in schedules and order, her whirlwind move to the States felt like someone had pushed her from a plane without handing her a parachute.

She needed a plan for how to land without completely losing herself.

Five days of Ian and his family in Melbourne. Five nights of him in her bed. Her head was still spinning . . . so much of it still felt surreal.

And now I'm in New York.

Looking at a condo I can't possibly afford.

Ian was waiting for her to say something.

"It's big," she said without stepping farther inside.

"It's yours." His tone was so calm, it took Claire a second to register what he'd said.

"It's lovely, but I can tell without asking that it's way outside my price range. Way, way out. Whatever realtor you're using needs to consider my finances rather than yours." She smoothed her hands down the sides of her skirt. "Don't be offended, but I should probably find my own realtor."

A funny smile spread across his face as he pulled an envelope out of his inside suit pocket. "That would be waste of time since you already own this place." He held out the envelope. "This is the deed to it."

The room spun.

Claire kept her hands at her sides. "No."

"Yes."

She shook her head. "You're joking."

He waved the envelope at her. "Take a look for yourself."

"I don't want it."

He frowned and lowered the envelope. "Not the reaction I expected."

"How much does a place like this cost?"

The corner of his mouth curled. "Didn't anyone ever tell you not to ask how much a gift cost?" He reached for her, but she took a step back.

"I'm serious."

He returned the envelope to his jacket pocket. "Talk to me, Claire."

She waved a hand through the air and tried to gather her thoughts. It was too much, too soon. "What if we're not even dating next week?" The question burst out of her and hung in the air between them.

All hints of a smile left his face. Their eyes met and held. She felt horrible about asking the question aloud, but now that it was out there . . . she held her breath waiting for his reaction.

"Do you see that happening?" he asked in a low tone.

Oh, God. "I don't know." They'd been virtually inseparable the past week, but in Claire's experience independence was the key to success. Remaining realistic and prepared to handle things on their own was what she advocated for her clients. Prenups. Non-disclosure agreements. When something was important, it was better to protect yourself, because everyone eventually disappointed you. She hadn't just preached that philosophy, she believed it. She lived it. "This is all happening so fast."

"There are no strings attached to this gift."

"Really?" she countered. "So, you're not expecting to stay here with me?"

He frowned.

She continued. "Did you give up your place? Is this where we both live now? Don't you think a move like that should be talked about first? Or did you keep your place? Like a backup plan? How convenient for you."

"Hey. Hey. Hey. Obviously, I did not think this through. I wanted to do something nice for you, and most women I know would—" He wisely stopped there. "I don't know what you want me to say."

"Clearly." She ran a hand through her hair and looked around the condo. It was beautiful. Modern. Comfortable. He'd probably paid several million dollars for it.

As foreign as the idea was to Claire, there probably were many women who wouldn't have had an issue with having such a condo bought for them. She was tempted to tell Ian she couldn't be bought—but was that what he was trying to do?

They'd promised to always be honest with each other. Dale had asked them to be kind as well. Claire took a deep breath and lowered her defenses. "The only relationship I want to be in is one where I feel like an equal partner. I can afford to rent my own apartment. Granted, it won't be in Upper Manhattan, but it'll still be nice." She softened her voice as she realized he was listening as openly as she was speaking. "I'll invite you over. And you can invite me to your place."

He gave her a long look. "Because we don't want to invest too much into something that might not be anything next week."

It sounded even worse when he said it. "I don't want us to end. I just need to be okay if we do."

He nodded once. "You do have trouble trusting people."

She remembered their exchange. "Especially when someone tells me they aren't good at relationships."

"I did say that."

"You did."

"Come here," he said, holding out his hand to her.

She wanted to, but she stayed where she was. "Maybe you should come *here*."

His eyes lit with humor. "Is that how it's going to be?"

Warmth spread through her even as she tossed more of his own words back at him. "I'm a lot. I get it. If you don't think you have what it takes to bring me to heel, I'll understand."

A laugh rumbled out of him, then his expression sobered. "I don't want to change you, Claire. You're pretty incredible the way you are."

She smiled. "So are you."

"Then maybe we should meet in the middle." His tone was so serious, but she recognized the look in his eyes, and suddenly her thoughts flooded with memories of his kiss, his touch, the feel of him wrapped around her as she came.

She stepped out of her shoes. "We could name this place THE MIDDLE." Then began to unbutton her blouse.

"I like that." He kicked off his shoes and tossed his jacket across the back of a chair. "A place for us to meet. You invite me. I invite you." He folded his shirt and placed it on his jacket, before reaching for the belt of his trousers.

She placed her own clothing neatly on the chair beside her without taking her eyes off him then stood before him, naked with chin held high. "I want this to work."

"So do I." He shed the last of his clothing. His cock was fully erect, but when he pulled her into his arms he simply held her for a moment. "I may have also cleared out an office for you in my building."

She hugged her arms around his waist and admitted to herself that she was more afraid than offended. When things felt too good to be true, they usually were. "Without asking me."

"I'm not used to answering to anyone."

She leaned her head back so she could look him in the eye. *This is who he is. He'll never be someone who dances to my tune, but would I want that? He's a man who knows what he wants, and he's used to getting it.*

Sometimes I think we're too different.

Other times I worry we're too similar.

I also know what I want, and I've never been afraid to go out and get it for myself.

She brought a hand up to caress his cheek. "What are you doing with someone like me?"

He tucked her hair behind her ears. "Falling hard."

We have that in common as well.

He kissed her and all desire for more talk disappeared. No matter what tomorrow brought, this was where she wanted to be. With Ian, she didn't feel wrong, even when she said something that would have become a full out argument with another man.

With him, she could be herself.

And it felt good.

As good as his hands felt as they gripped her ass and lifted her off the ground.

Her phone buzzed with an incoming message. She ignored it and writhed against Ian.

His beeped as well.

Hers again.

Then his.

Fuck.

She broke off the kiss. "We should check just to make sure it's not an emergency."

He groaned. "You're right." He leaned over with her still wrapped around his waist to check the caller ID on his phone. "It's Kade."

Hands on his shoulders, she clung to him. "My phone is right—"

He took a step and leaned so they could both see the face of her phone. "Annie," they said in unison.

Both of their phones began to ring. "It might be something important," Claire said, slowly lowering her feet to the ground.

"It had better be," he growled.

Claire answered her phone as Ian stepped away to answer his. God, he looked as good from the rear as he did from the front. Were those marks on his back from her? *What a perfectly rounded ass. It makes me want to take a little bite.*

"Claire? You there?"

Claire shook her head. *Annie. Oh, yeah.* "Hey, welcome back. Is something wrong?"

"Wrong? Maybe. Wildly unexpected—for sure. Are you and Ian a couple now?"

"We are." It still felt strange to say it.

"I go on one honeymoon and everything changes. What happened? I wasn't even aware you liked him. And he definitely didn't seem to like you. We'd heard he was in Melbourne having dinner with my parents. Now you and Ian are all Sophie and Dale are talking about. I need to know what's going on. Can you talk now?"

Claire glanced at Ian who did not look pleased with the conversation he was having. "Not really."

"Ian's there?"

"Yes, but he's on the phone too."

"Oh, God. I hope Kade didn't call him. You should have

seen his face when Sophie announced you were seeing Ian and moving to New York to date him."

"Ian's not the only reason—" Claire stopped herself. He wasn't, but he was the main reason. There was no need to try to disguise that with Annie. "Why doesn't Kade want to see me with Ian?"

"It's more like he doesn't want to see Ian with you. Let's face it, Ian hasn't handled Kade returning as well as the rest of the family has. Kade doesn't trust him. Should he? You tell me. You're dating Ian now—has he changed? Is he over the crazy idea that Pamela might be a horrible person?"

Claire brought a shaking hand up to her mouth. They'd talked about it. She'd shared how she felt about revenge. It had been a good talk, but had it changed his mind? "I don't know," she said in a thick voice.

"Oh, Claire. I would love for you and Ian to work out. I mean, we'd finally really be sisters. But if he finds something on Pamela, Kade will protect her. She has always been so good to him. Regardless of how he came into her life, in his heart, she's his mother. The fear that Ian might try to hurt her while we were gone was a dark cloud on our honeymoon. I was much more sympathetic to Ian's anger before I realized how deeply it's hurting Kade. Now I just want to kick his ass."

"I'm sorry, Annie."

"No, I'm sorry I can't celebrate you being with Ian. If he tries to take down Pamela, it'll tear Kade apart, and I can't imagine him ever being part of our lives again. If you're with him . . ."

Claire suddenly felt a little sick. "He's a good man, Annie. No matter what he found out, he would do what's best for his family and that includes Kade."

"Do you really believe that?" Annie asked, her voice revealing her relief.

"Yes," Claire said with more conviction than she felt.

Sex was great.

Laughing together was nice.

The way he listened intently when Claire spoke was heartwarming.

But when it came right down to it, she didn't know if her opinion had swayed him at all.

"I'll call you back," Claire said, ending her call with Annie. She lowered the phone and turned her attention to Ian.

His face was contorted with anger, and he growled, "I don't respond well to threats, Kade."

Their eyes met and she silently pleaded him to soften. *Don't do this. Be the man I know you are, not the one Annie fears you could be.*

There was a change in his expression—anger twisted to pain. Still he didn't look away. Despite the distance between them, and that Kade's harsh response was loud enough that Ian moved the phone a few inches from his ear, Claire felt very much connected to Ian in that moment.

He hears me.

Come on, Ian. I know you love your brother.

Holding his gaze as she approached, Claire walked over and slipped beneath one of his arms. She'd already said what she thought, but she also wanted him to know she felt his pain. She hugged him, bare skin to bare skin, and laid her head on his chest. His heart was beating so loudly she knew none of this was easy for him.

He hugged her closer, tucking her beneath his chin for a moment. In the silence, Kade's voice reached both of them easily.

"It's not enough for you to go after the woman who raised me. Not enough to be a prick at my wedding. I leave Boston for a couple of weeks, and you decide to have dinner with Annie's parents? Make a play for her best friend? Are you hoping to find something on them as well? Why? What is so twisted up in your head that you need to fuck with me and mine? And don't give me any shit about this being about what happened to me. This is all about you, although for the life of me I can't figure out what the fuck you think you'll get out of wrecking my life. Do you want my share of the inheritance back? Fucking take it."

"This isn't about money," Ian said in a tight voice.

"I don't care what it's about anymore. Stay the hell away from Annie, Pamela, and anyone associated with either of them. I'm not a violent man, but I swear to God if you hurt any of them I'll kill you. On the upside? I can now afford a good defense lawyer."

The call ended and neither Claire nor Ian took a breath for a long moment.

Eventually Ian said, "So, that was my call. How did yours go?"

Before she'd slept with Ian, before he'd truly let her in, Claire would have interpreted his cool tone and his joke as arrogance or indifference. She knew him too well for that, though. The man in her arms was tense. His breathing was shallow. Jaw clenched. He was hurting.

So she simply held him for a moment longer, before saying, "Annie said Kade wasn't thrilled to hear we're together."

A laugh rumbled in his chest, and he kissed her forehead. "You think?"

She took a leap of faith. "He won't trust you until he sees the man I know you are. You need to tell him you love him and you value your relationship with him more than whatever happened thirty years ago. He needs to hear it."

Ian shuddered against Claire. "I really fucked this up."

She leaned her head back to meet his eyes. "There is no manual for how to respond when you hear the brother you thought was dead was actually kidnapped and raised by another family. People might say they'd know how to handle it, but no one really could unless they faced that kind of trauma. And that's what happened to you. Life gave you a real nut twist and you kicked out at it. I understand. But now that you know your kick hurt the same people you wish you could have protected—what are you going to do about it?"

He let out an audible breath. "I'm going to apologize and stop looking for what will only hurt them more if I find it." Then he smiled. "A nut twist?"

"Can you imagine anything more painful?" She arched an eyebrow.

He shook his head and chuckled. "No, I can't." Then his expression changed, turning almost tender. "Well, one thing."

He didn't say what that one thing was, and she didn't ask. She knew what she hoped he thought would hurt more. Every day she was with him it became harder and harder to imagine her life without him.

He kissed her lips gently then asked, "What do you say we head up to Boston on Saturday? I'll ask Kenzi to organize a game night. We'll go, show them I'm not with you for any nefarious reason, and I'll talk to Kade on the side."

She wound her arms around his neck. "If you're not sure what to say, I can help you plan it out."

"I'm sure you can," he joked. "Words are something you're never in short supply of."

She gave the back of his neck a playful smack. "Better take that back."

"I would, but what I have in mind for the rest of the night has nothing to do with talking." He swung her up in his arms. "There are two bedrooms. Do you have a preference?"

Inspired as well as turned on, Claire suggested, "I believe in making informed decisions. I'll need to try both before I choose."

He looked down at her with fire burning in his eyes. "Once you choose—I bet it's forever."

She traced the outline of his strong chin. "I bet you're the same."

At the edge of a bed, Ian stopped and searched her face. "How do you have more faith in me than I have in myself?"

There was so much she could have said, but he was looking emotionally ragged after the call from Kade. Time to lighten the mood. "We could have a good, long discussion about that, but I thought your plans included *not talking*."

A sexy grin spread across his face. "Oh, yes." He laid her gently on the bed, then joined her, looking into her eyes while playfully tracing her lips. "One day I might not even yearn for duct tape."

"Shut up and kiss me."

They both laughed through that first deep kiss.

Chapter Thirteen

A FEW DAYS later, Ian parked in front of his parents' home, gripped the steering wheel, and inhaled sharply. He'd faced down violent dictators, toppled mafia kings, even taken a life a few times when it was the only way to defend the innocent—and he'd done it all without hesitation.

Because I used to trust my instincts.

I was sure I was on the right side, so whatever happened was worth the risk.

This time I was wrong, maybe not about Pamela's character, but about how much the truth was worth. I told myself it was all for my family, but Kade is right . . . it was for my own fucked up agenda.

I wanted to put right what cannot be changed.

I wanted it more than I cared who it hurt.

Life gave my nuts a twist and I kicked back.

He released his seat belt and glanced at Claire, who seemed remarkably calm. She either didn't know he was freaking the fuck out, or she was being strong for him—either way she was exactly what he needed right then.

Needed. It was a novel feeling for him.

People turned to him in crisis. He was the fixer. Everyone's Hail Mary pass. Before her he would have said he didn't need anyone.

In response to his sustained attention, she smiled in support. "When you get Kade alone, start with 'I love you.' It's hard to have a knockdown fight with someone who does that." When he didn't immediately agree, she added, "He's not happy with you. And he has a right to be upset. Tell him you care even though he won't believe you. Not today."

"I love your optimism," he said dryly.

She cocked her head to one side. "Oh, I thought you could handle the truth. I'm sorry. Go on in there, Tiger, and hug it out. I'm fifteen percent positive that won't get you a punch to the face. Sorry, there I go again preparing you for reality. You handle this any way you want. I'm sure it'll work out fine."

He sought her hand with his and brought it to his lips. "He's not going to punch me."

Her eyes darkened. "I know. You can do this, Ian. Your hand is cold though. Is your heart racing? Do you have adrenaline pumping through you?"

He could have denied it. Would have with anyone but her. "Yes."

She laced her fingers through his. "That's how you know this is important. It's also how I know I made the right choice to come with you. You love your family. When they needed a warrior, you fought for them. They need something else now, a different kind of strength from you."

His throat clenched with emotion. He swallowed hard.

"I understand now why your clients are willing to pay you so well. When you look at me like that, I feel . . ."

A loud knock on the window was followed by a second.

Ian groaned when two big, blond goons appeared at his car window. When he saw one about to knock again, he lowered his window. "Dylan. Connor. I had no idea you'd be here this weekend."

"Game night. We hate to miss them," Connor said with a huge grin, as if Ian's greeting had been a warm one. He reached inside the car and waved at Claire. "Hey, coach. What do you think of my suit?"

Claire whistled. "Looks tailor made."

"It was. Clay had us measured for them so we'll blend in when we go to New York. Turns out Dylan and I are almost exactly the same size, except in the crotch. He had to have that area taken in. If you don't use it, you lose it. Sad, really." He made a pained sound and swayed to the side from a punch Dylan gave him to the shoulder.

Dylan's face replaced Connors in the open window. "Don't listen to him, Claire. He's full of shit. And he thinks he's funny, but he's not. If he doesn't stop lying about the fitting, I'm going to prove just how delusional he is."

"Please don't," Claire said, looking as if she was fighting back a smile.

They don't annoy her. She actually does like them.

As Dylan and Connor scuffled a bit to claim time in the window, Ian found himself smiling as well. The meatheads were harmless, really. And funny when he saw them through Claire's eyes.

They were also kind of related since they were the brothers of Viviana, Grant's wife. An uncle, just like him, to their child.

Family.

He only realized he'd said it out loud when Connor repeated the word. "Did you hear him, Dylan? He just called us family." The door was thrown open.

"This calls for a hug," Connor proclaimed, dragging Ian out of the car. Although he'd been trained in self-defense, there was a certain amount of disbelief in dealing with Dylan and Connor that gave them the advantage. Short of delivering a painful strike, there wasn't much Ian could do but accept the hug that lifted him clear off his feet. "Thanks for not being angry about our little prank at the wedding. I told Dylan you were cool, but he thought you might put a hit out on us."

"Get your hands off me," Ian said in a firm voice.

Claire's laughter rang out from beside them. "Connor, put him down."

Normally Ian would have been irritated, but when he looked at Claire he was temporarily taken by her bright smile. Her eyes were dancing, and he fell just a little bit more in love with her.

"Give him a hug, Dylan," Connor said.

"I don't hug men," Dylan protested.

"I hug everyone," Connor said. "Look at Ian. He's smiling. See, doesn't matter who gives it, a hug is good for the soul."

"I'm still not hugging him." Dylan put his hands on his

hips.

Ian straightened his jacket. "And that makes you my favorite meathead."

Dylan and Connor exchanged a look then both smiled. Connor added, "Ian, you seem a lot happier now that you're getting laid. Whatever you're doing, Claire, keep it up."

She burst out laughing.

Ian shook his head. They were growing on him, but he leaned in, placed a hand on the back of each of their necks, and pulled their heads closer so they could hear him say, "We're good, but if you talk about Claire like that again, I'll break both your legs. You'll be hugging everyone from a wheelchair."

"Sorry, Claire," they both said in unison once released.

Then Dylan frowned. "Hey, I didn't even say anything."

"It's guilt by allocation," Connor said with confidence.

Ian coughed back a laugh. "Guilt by *association*."

Dylan went to punch his brother in the arm again. "See what happens when you fill your head with too many big words. You don't even use them right."

Connor caught Dylan's fist in his hand. "I'm thinking about going to college with the money we make from the movie. You stay a dumb ass. I might become a doctor or scientist or some shit like that."

A few weeks ago, Ian would have laughed right along with Dylan at the idea of Connor making that kind of change, but there was an earnestness about him that made Ian want something good to happen for him. "If you need someone to go with you to check out college campuses—"

He wanted to offer to do it. Claire looked like she expected him to. He opened his mouth to, then said, "Asher loves that kind of stuff. And Andrew's wife is taking college courses now so she could speak to the experience of getting a degree later in life."

He met Claire's gaze and mouthed, "I tried."

She took his hand and mouthed back, "Baby steps. Proud of you."

From the door of the house, Viviana called out, "Dylan. Connor. Dale is setting up a volleyball net, but he looks like he needs help."

"On it," Dylan said.

"Coming," Connor called back.

As they walked away, Dylan said, "Connor, I was just joking. You should go to college if you want to."

"Thanks," Connor said, putting his arm around his brother's shoulders.

"Your dick will always be smaller than mine, but you could console yourself with being smarter."

Connor's hug turned to a neck hold and a noogie on the top of Dylan's head. "Maybe I'll become a brain surgeon and we'll finally figure out what's wrong with yours."

"Never tell anyone about their little 'prank,'" Ian said, as he hugged Claire to his side.

"I'll take it to my grave, but they might not," she said with a smile. She glanced up at him. "Grant and Viviana know, too. They like you, though, so who knows."

"As long as no one tells Asher—" Ian started.

"Tells Asher what?" Asher asked from beside them.

When Ian and Claire looked at him without answering, Asher said, "Fine, keep your secrets. I came out to warn you that things are a little tense inside. You might want to tone down the whole Pamela shit."

Asher could be such an ass, but whenever Ian needed him—he had his back. "I appreciate the heads up. I have a plan."

"A plan?" Asher asked as if that didn't sound like a good thing. "Want to run it by me first?"

Claire raised a hand. "Asher, I love you."

Asher's eyebrows rose. "Well, this is awkward. I'm very much taken."

She wagged a finger at Asher, but her tone was serious. "You're the perfect one to help Ian this weekend."

In his life, Ian had probably seen Asher speechless only once . . . and that was the night Emily's museum had burned to the ground. It was almost entertaining to see him not sure what to say. Finally, he cleared his throat and said, "Anything."

Ian nodded. This felt right. "I plan to take Kade aside and tell him he has nothing to worry about from me."

"Okay, and then?"

Ian rubbed the back of his neck. "I'll explain to him that I'm serious about Claire." He exchanged a look with Claire and smiled. "And hopefully not get punched."

At his announcement, Claire's face went pink, so beautiful Ian couldn't look away.

Asher folded his arms over his chest. "I couldn't picture the two of you together, but I get it now. I guess. You've got the old '*I hate you, hate you, don't trust you, hang on, you're kind of hot, let's do this*' vibe."

Claire laughed. "Asher, you're a master of summary. That's exactly what happened."

Ian frowned. He liked to think there was a little more to them than that, but that was a topic for another time.

Asher shrugged. "I am intuitive. I tell Emily all the time I could be a relationship therapist if I gave a shit about other people."

Ian barked out a laugh.

Claire joined in.

"Not that funny." Asher's tone was serious, but there was a hint of humor in his eyes. "Let's go see if you can peel Kade off the ceiling. Something about having dinner with Annie's parents while he was on his honeymoon really pissed him off." He paused halfway up the stairs. "Seriously, that was low even for you."

"I didn't do it because—" Ian began to say he hadn't gone to Melbourne to see them, but he stopped. This wasn't about winning an argument, or defending himself, it was about apologizing for not seeing how much he was hurting those around him. "I love you, Asher," he said, and winked at Claire.

Asher froze and turned. "Neither of you are high, right? If you are, just say it. I'll tell Mom and Dad you have malaria or something. But don't go in there and fuck up worse."

"Not high, just happy." Ian and Claire stopped just in front of Asher. Ian said, "I've got this, Asher."

"He's got this," Claire echoed.

CLAIRE PAUSED BEFORE walking through the front door and gripped Ian's hand tightly. An emotional lump clogged her throat. For months Sophie and Dale's home had felt like her own. They'd not only asked her to stay with them when she'd come to Boston to help Annie and Kade—they'd told her it was where she belonged.

Belonged.

As a child she'd yearned to have a place like that.

As an adult she'd told herself it was overrated. Unlike many of her friends, holidays were stress free for her. No bickering siblings. No parents with crazy high expectations. She was free.

And lonely.

She saw that now.

Inside that door a storm was brewing, and she was walking in holding the hand of the man at the center of it. If this went badly, she could lose Annie, her place at her parents' table, all of it.

Annie's fears came back to Claire then. If Kade couldn't bear to be around Ian . . .

She took a calming breath. *If Annie stops talking to me because Ian pisses off Kade, it doesn't say much about our friendship. I can't let that be what guides me here.*

I don't want to choose a side.

Ian dipped his head down to near her ear. "Having second thoughts?"

"No, just getting my head in a good place in case this doesn't go well."

He took a moment before saying, "My family cares about

you, Claire. I'm the one they're not happy with."

She digested his words but didn't like how they made her feel. "I've never been serious enough about anyone to get close to their family, but I already love yours. Annie told me she's worried that if you and Kade have problems . . ."

"That you and she will."

"Yes." Claire chewed her lip absently then said, "I don't accept that. If you argue with Kade today, that won't make me hate him. If Annie can't separate her feelings for me from this, it says something unflattering about our friendship, doesn't it?"

His eyes darkened. "You don't have to come in with me."

Her back straightened. "Oh, I'm going in."

"After you prepare yourself to handle when you discover that none of them actually care about you."

How did he see her so clearly? Her response was a choked whisper, "Yes."

He pulled her to him for a hug. She expected him to say something, but he didn't. He simply held her. And she soaked in his strength. In his arms was another place that felt like everything she'd tried to convince herself she didn't need.

In that moment she realized the idea of losing him was a hundred times scarier than never talking to Annie again. She shivered at the thought. Leaving herself that vulnerable to anyone was just begging to have her heart broken.

She'd sworn she'd never let anyone have the power to hurt her that deeply again.

Yet, here I am falling in love with a man who is as bad at relationships as I am.

Is there any version of this that doesn't end like a train wreck?

From the doorway, Dale said, "Oh, good, you're here. Before you come in—"

"I know, Dad," Ian said over Claire's head. She stepped out of his arms.

"Hi, Dale."

"Hi, Claire." Dale sighed. "Why don't you go in and give me a minute with Ian?"

Ian pocketed his hands. "Go on in, Claire. He's not going to say anything you need to hear again."

Claire didn't move. She didn't want to choose sides, but neutrality wasn't likely going to be an option that day. She raised her chin and met Dale's eyes. "I'm here with Ian." Then she turned to Ian. "If you want a moment alone with your father, of course I'll go in. I'd rather walk through that door together, though. You have some things to apologize for, but being with me shouldn't be one of them."

Ian held her gaze, then nodded and held out his hand.

She took it without hesitation.

Dale cleared his throat. "So you know, Kade is upset."

"Asher gave us a heads-up," Ian said.

"We've tried to explain to him that meeting with Annie's parents was our idea, but he doesn't believe it." Dale looked tired, and it was hard not to worry that the stress of this might affect him.

Ian squared his shoulders. "I've given him reason not to

trust me. I'll talk to him, Dad. That's why we're here." Dale seemed to be waiting for more and got it when Ian added, "Nothing in the past is more important than what we have today. It took me a while to understand that, but I do now."

A slow smile spread across Dale's face. "You mean that?"

Ian nodded. "I do."

Relief flooded Dale's face. "You have no idea how good it feels to hear that." He turned a stern look toward Claire. "I do have a problem with you, though, young lady."

Claire's eyebrows shot up. "Me?"

Then he smiled again. "Where's my hug?"

Tears filled her eyes, but she blinked them back and stepped away from Ian long enough to greet Dale properly. Sophie appeared behind him, so Claire hugged her tightly as well.

I'm doing a horrible job at protecting my heart from these Barringtons.

But maybe that's not such a bad thing.

When she returned to Ian's side and his strong hand linked with hers again, she let out a shaky breath. Life was less terrifying when she didn't care this deeply for anyone, but that wasn't how she wanted to live anymore.

I do fear that people will leave me.

But if I were one of my own clients I'd tell myself, "Fear is just nature's way of saying something is important."

She met Ian's gaze for a long moment. *You're important to me.*

So is your family.

And what we have is worth fighting for.

So let's go face this storm.

"Are we doing this?" Claire prompted with forced humor.

Ian's expression remained serious. "Yes, we are."

Hand in hand, they followed Dale into the house.

Chapter Fourteen

THE GENERAL MOOD inside his parents' home wasn't better or worse than Ian expected. No voices were raised in anger. People weren't visibly arguing. There was, however, a noticeable lack of smiles and laughter.

Game night was about gathering and having fun. Asher's wife, Emily, had started the tradition, and it had become a way his family connected. This time, however, there were no children in attendance. That wasn't a good sign.

Kade and Annie froze when he and Claire entered the living room. Neither of them looked happy. Ian greeted the rest of his siblings as he made his way across the room, but there wasn't a good conversation that would happen with any of them until he settled things with Kade.

Kade stood as he and Claire approached. Ian looked on in approval when Annie left his brother's side to embrace her. Regardless of how this went down, Claire deserved a friend who would love her regardless. Annie was damn lucky to have someone like Claire on her side, and if she didn't see that . . . it would truly be her loss.

No need to dance around why he'd come. "Kade, we

need to talk."

"I said everything I intend to," Kade said in a cold tone.

"I haven't." Ian glanced around. "This conversation might be best had in private."

Kade shook his head. "Why? Do you have something to say you don't want them to know? If you think you've got something on me, lay it on me, right here. Let everyone see exactly who you are."

Sophie moved to intervene. "Kade, Ian isn't—"

Dale cut her off. "Sophie, they need to work it out on their own."

Ian looked around the room again. All of his siblings were standing in silent audience with their spouses. Asher and his wife Emily. Grant and Viviana. Lance and Willa. Kenzi and Dax. Even Andrew and his wife Helene who must have flown up from Florida.

Because that's what we do—we pull together in times of crisis.

This time, however, I'm the crisis.

They think I'm about to tear our family apart.

Ian remembered what Claire had said about them needing a different kind of strength from him. His parents didn't need him to find Kade—he was already back. Kade didn't need to be protected—he was already safe.

Ian took a moment to exchange a look with Claire. Did she know how much she'd affected his view of the world already? Without her, he would have interpreted this scene as everyone siding against him.

They're not.

They're here to fight for the peace our family has finally found.

And they need me to show them I'm willing to fight for the same thing.

He silently thanked Claire for helping him realize that.

She smiled gently. She believed in him.

God, sometimes it's like I can feel her thoughts.

Ian turned back to Kade. Annie was once again at his side, holding his hand in support. *His ride-or-die partner.*

Claire slipped her hand in Ian's. He smiled without taking his eyes off Kade. *I never thought I'd have one as well. So, here goes, Claire. This one is for you.* "I love you, Kade, and I'm sorry for the way I've been behaving."

Kade's eyes narrowed. "Is this some kind of game?"

"No, this is me saying I was wrong. I wanted to make sense of something that doesn't make sense. Will never make sense. I wanted to punish someone because I needed to feel that I had done something in the face of that. I didn't see how it was hurting you."

Kade continued to glare at Ian.

Ian continued, "That's not true. I did see it. I simply didn't think it was as important as finding someone to blame. I haven't done much to show it, but I do care about you, and I'm glad you're back in our lives. I understand it will take you time to believe me, but no one you care about has anything to fear from me. From now on I'll be the brother I should have been from the beginning."

Claire hugged his arm to her side.

The room remained painfully silent for several long moments.

The ball was in Kade's court.

Would he accept the olive branch Ian was offering him?

Just then, Connor and Dylan burst into the room. Dylan announced, "Volleyball net put up. Check. Horseshoes' posts in lawn. Check. We went a step further and set up for croquet. Had to look that shit up on our phones. The game sounds really boring, but you do have beer, right?"

When no one said anything, Connor looked around. "What happened?"

Still nothing.

Then Asher called out, "Ian just told Kade he loves him."

Connor brought a hand to his heart. "And I missed it." He walked over to Ian.

Ian put a splayed hand in his direction. "Don't do it."

Connor looked back and forth between Ian and Kade and frowned. "Brothers are tough. No one can cut you deeper, but no one can make you laugh as hard either. I know how to make you laugh, Kade."

Viviana rushed across the room. "Connor, why don't you help me start bringing food outside."

Dylan piped in, "Do it, Connor, if you have the balls to."

Both of Ian's hands went up and he took a step back. "Seriously, Connor, not now." He glanced at Claire. She was fighting back a smile. *Oh, really. And she claims to have my back?*

With ninja-like speed, Connor picked Ian up again and shook him with a bone-crushing hug. "Ian is really just a softy. When he growls at you, Kade, all he's really saying is that he needs a hug."

"Holy shit," Andrew said.

"Watch your language, Andrew," Dale reprimanded.

"I'm so sorry, Ian," Viviana said. "Connor. Stop it right now. This isn't funny."

Ian was completely in agreement until he heard Kade start to laugh. Everyone else slowly joined in. Claire was laughing so hard she was wiping tears from her eyes.

Still crushed to Connor's chest, Ian said, "You do realize I could hurt you if I wanted to."

Connor lowered him back to his feet, grinning like an idiot. "But you won't because we're family." He turned toward Kade who was still laughing. "All of us."

"I love your brothers," Grant called out from across the room.

It was all the encouragement Connor needed to reach for Kade. "Bring it in."

Kade evaded him, but this time Ian was the one who was laughing. "Come on, Kade. Everyone needs a hug now and then."

They shared their first nonconfrontational look, and it felt good.

Sophie walked over and tapped Connor on the arm. "I'd love one, Connor."

He lifted her up and swung her around with such enthusiasm the room collectively held their breath until she let out a laugh of delight. When he returned her to her feet near Dale, she said, "I considered myself blessed when I thought I had seven children, but my family just keeps growing, and I couldn't be happier. I know you're technically not a Barrington, Connor, but I want you to know you can call me Mom if you want to."

Dylan was at her side in a heartbeat. "Both of us?"

She pulled Dylan to her for a hug. "Of course. You are both a source of light and joy for us. Don't ever change. We could all learn a lot from you."

Both Dylan and Connor went beet red, but they looked pleased.

Sophie did as well.

Ian looked around the room again. Smiles had returned. Some were still chuckling. Viviana was the only one who looked uncertain, and Ian understood that he was the one who had the power to change that. "Come here, Dylan. You look like you need a hug."

Dylan took a step back.

Ian stepped closer. "Come on, bring it in."

Dylan moved so both Sophie and Dale were between them. "Hell no."

He took a step to go around his parents and enjoyed how Dylan retreated to the other side of Sophie. "This is more fun than I thought," Ian joked and gave Connor a punch to the arm—one that would have hurt most men, but didn't even get a flinch from the giant.

Connor smiled and punched him back. "Right?"

It fucking hurt, too, but Ian stood his ground and smiled. "Right," he ground out.

Kade stepped forward, filling Ian's view. "I want to trust

this version of you."

Not a version of me. Just me. The me I should have been from the start. "I understand that it'll take time, but that's something we have."

Kade nodded. "I've never seen you smile so much."

Ian reached a hand out toward Claire. She ducked beneath his arm, wrapping hers around his waist. "I recently started working with an accountability coach who is helping me view things in a fresh light."

Kade put an arm around Annie's waist. "I do remember thinking she'd be good for you."

"You did?" Ian found that surprising.

Annie interjected. "She was the only woman we could imagine who could take you down a notch."

Ian glanced down at Claire. "Is that your plan for me?"

Without missing a beat, Claire replied, "Only one notch? No."

They shared a smile that had his heart doing a funny flip, but he warned her, "No one ever really changes."

She held his gaze. "I don't want you to."

His smile widened. "I don't want you to, either."

From Sophie's side, Dylan bravely said, "Touching as this is to watch, did you say the beer was in the main fridge or the pool house?"

Lance waved toward the door. "Willa and I will help you find some, Dylan. Since the twins are with a babysitter today, we may join you in a few." He directed his next comment to his wife. "Am I the only one who saw this going much worse?"

Asher said, "Em, you want one? I could use a drink too."

Emily nodded. "Please."

None of them had ever been beer drinkers, but when Dylan and Connor were present it was slowly becoming his siblings' beverage of choice. Possibly because neither of the meatheads handled hard liquor well.

Sophie raised a hand. "They're in the pool house. Please bring me back one as well."

The room fell into stunned silence.

His mother hardly drank at all, but when she did it was champagne or a white wine. Beer? Who were these people? As if realizing her request might have shocked her family, she shrugged and said, "Annie's parents sent over some of their craft brews, and they're actually quite nice. Healthy too. Even your father's doctor approves of them."

Dale added, "On that note, bring me back one as well."

"Claire?" Ian asked.

She smiled first at him then at Annie. "Absolutely. I practically grew up on the stuff. I doubt the States have anything that compares."

"Are you laying down a challenge?" Ian definitely wasn't a beer drinker, but this was a matter of patriotism.

"Have you tried Mitch and Hazel's craft brews?"

"Not yet."

Kade slapped a hand on Ian's back. "Well, then, mate, let's see how you hold your own against those of us who can drink it like water." He paused for effect. "Unless you're afraid."

"Afraid? No," Ian said with full confidence then ducked

to whisper into Claire's ear, "I don't normally drink. Pull me out if you see this going bad."

She kissed him lightly on the lips. "I've got you, babe."

A few hours later, Claire was on a bench in the backyard still nursing a glass of water, watching Ian laugh his way through a game of croquet with Kade, Dylan, and Connor. After Dylan and Connor had introduced chaser shots to the beer drinking, one by one the others had reached their max and headed inside. Ian, however, refused to stop before the others did. He swayed as he lined up his mallet for his shot, but that was the only sign so far that he was drunk as a skunk.

That and the perma-smile on his face.

Annie came to sit beside her. "Hey."

Claire bumped shoulders with her. "Hey."

"I'm sorry about what I said the other day. I was frustrated. What I should have said was thank you for all you've done for me . . . especially these last few months . . . and nothing will ever change that; in my heart, you're my sister."

Blinking back tears, Claire sniffed. "Thank you; let's put that behind us. Even sisters argue."

Annie put an arm around Claire. "I really couldn't picture you and Ian together, but now that I've seen it, I can. He's changing because of you."

Was he? "I hope not. We met him at a bad time so you don't have the best impression of him, but Grant told me Ian was always the one calling to make sure they gathered when Sophie needed them to. Lance told me Ian was always on him about his grades—checking in to make sure he did well and if he didn't, Ian found him tutors. Do you know he's the one who taught Kenzi to drive? He flies down to see Andrew on a regular basis to make sure he's still sober and has someone to talk to when he needs it. When I look at Ian, I see someone who has always tried to be who he thought his family needed him to be. He loves them very much and with a loyalty I wish my own family had shown me."

"You're right, I don't know that side of him. Kade doesn't either."

"Hopefully you'll both see it now." Claire watched Kade take a poor shot that was blatantly a result of how much beer he'd imbibed in. Ian said something to him that made him smile, and then he did a similarly bad shot that had Kade hooting triumphantly.

"I hope so," Annie sighed. "What a wild ride this has been."

Now that was something Claire could agree with. "It sure has been."

"Are you living with Ian?"

"No, I found a place of my own—a studio down in the Financial District. We're not ready for any big steps. But I am renting an office in his building. He didn't want me to pay, but it's important to me that I do. He's used to people wanting something from him. I want to be with him, but I want to know that if he left me tomorrow, I could stand on my own two feet. That's important to me."

Annie's eyes darkened. "Claire, I didn't know that spending time in Boston was affecting your business."

"I wish you didn't know now. It's water under the

bridge, anyway. I'm starting fresh."

She gripped Annie's arm. "It's not to me. Kade and I were so wrapped up in what was going on in his life, then the wedding, neither of us thought to ask how it was affecting you."

"I'm a big girl, Annie. If I'd wanted to go home, I would have. The truth is I was done with that life, but I wasn't willing to admit it to myself yet."

Annie smiled. "Well, say what you will, I'm grateful and if I can figure out how to, I'm going to make sure something incredible happens for you."

Claire took her hand and gave it a squeeze. "Please don't. I'm fine. Dylan and Connor head down to New York next week. They're paying clients. I have connections already in the city. It won't take me long to build a clientele. This time, though, I'm going to schedule things more carefully. I'm seeking balance."

Annie laid her head on Claire's shoulder. "Did I tell you how good it feels to have you here?"

"No, but I'm hoping it's as good as it feels to be here."

A commotion across the yard drew both women's attention. The men had moved next to the pool. Dylan and Connor had stripped down to their boxers. Connor did a cannonball off the diving board. Dylan followed with a huge splash. They were both daring Kade and Ian to follow suit. Ian swayed and scratched his head as if considering it.

Claire stood. "I'm going to save Ian now. Call me tomorrow."

"I will," Annie promised, rising to her feet as well. As

they made their way toward the pool, Kade shed his clothes to his boxers and, all things considered, executed a rather impressive dive. "Oh, no. Kade, no." She looked around. "At least Sophie and Dale are inside."

"Ian," Claire called out. "Keep your pants—"

He waved her off, shed his suit, and performed a dive that would have made a Navy SEAL proud.

What was a woman to do? Claire took out her phone and videotaped the next round of dives the four men did. She might not be able to save him, but his ass was going to watch this the next day.

"What's all the noise?" Sophie asked from the door. "Oh. My." was all she said before she turned and went back into the house.

Claire and Annie exchanged a look and both burst out laughing. Claire said, "I'm guessing this is not how a Barrington house party normally turns out."

Her friend was still laughing as she agreed.

A moment later Asher and Grant appeared like bouncers sent in to settle a crowd. Grant shook his head as Ian did a flip off the side of the pool that ended in what sounded like a painful belly flop. He covered his eyes when Kade attempted a better version and almost landed on Ian's head.

"Okay," Asher called out. "Party's over. You're scaring Mom. None of you are driving yourselves anywhere, and all of you need to put some fucking clothes on."

With no warning, Grant gave Asher a push that sent him, suit and all, flying into the pool. "Yes," Ian said.

"You go, Grant," Connor encouraged before doing another belly flop.

Grant turned toward Annie and Claire and grinned. "I may be a little more drunk than I look."

Asher was swearing when he surfaced.

Everyone else was laughing.

Not to be outdone, Claire called out, "Don't worry, I caught it on video."

Ian whooped. "That's my woman right there."

"You're all assholes," Asher muttered as he made his way out of the pool, but no one seemed bothered by it. He stopped in front of Claire who was still videotaping. "Someone needs to show these fools how to do a proper dive."

With that, he stripped off his suit and headed for the diving board. Annie waved to Grant. "Go get Emily—quick! She needs to see this."

"Oh, I'm here," Emily said with a chuckle. "What's in Australian beer?" She sat down beside Annie. "Claire, you're getting all this, right?"

"Absolutely. They were fine until they started doing shots. At least they stopped at the boxers."

Helene, Andrew's wife, came out of the house laughing and dragging him behind her. Willa and Lance made their way to the side of the pool as well.

Helene joked, "Are you going to let them think that's how diving is done?"

"I'm way too sober to join them," Andrew said firmly.

"Someone has to get in there and make sure they don't drown. Who better than a Marine?"

Oh, she's good.

Andrew's resistance melted away beneath his wife's sweet look. He tossed his clothing on a chair and dove in with precision.

Lance gave Willa a kiss, stripped down to his—Superman boxers—and did an enthusiastic flip off the side of the pool that gained him a round of applause from the ladies watching. The Barrington men had calendar pinup bodies. Claire doubted any of the women would have said watching them frolic bare-chested was a hardship.

It was more of a feat not to drool.

Viviana undid Grant's tie and tossed it to the ground. "Get your ass in there too." He kissed her, and shed his suit as well, then dove in smoothly.

Kenzi and Dax were the last to appear outside. Dax didn't look the least bit interested in joining in, but he did say, "Clay is going to be sorry he missed today."

Claire stopped taping. "Barringtons gone wild. I could sell this video."

"I'll take a copy," Annie said.

"Forward me one as well," Emily said. "It would be the perfect blackmail video if they didn't look so damn good."

Helene laughed. "Don't let them hear you say that. Their egos are healthy enough. I have to say, though, Andrew was worried when we flew up. He doesn't like confrontation. Seeing them like this makes me so happy."

Annie gave Claire's hand a squeeze. "Now they look like a family. This is what I wanted for Kade."

"Me too. They're all going to be so hungover tomorrow, though," Emily said. "Even Asher, although he was trying to tell me he wasn't drunk. Hey, at least they all seem to have good taste in underclothing. It could be much worse."

In a soft voice, Willa said, "If you can *not* make too big a deal of Lance's . . . he's a little sensitive about his superhero collection."

"I'll edit it out," Claire promised.

Dax threw a ball into the pool and the sloppiest game of volleyball erupted. More spiking than skill, and what they considered the net was a mystery to Claire.

When Dax returned to where the women were gathered, his wife, Kenzi, came to stand beside him. He said, "This is good for them. They need more memories like this." He looked at the pool again, frowned, and added, "Maybe not exactly like this . . . but you get the idea."

"Sure you don't want to join them?" Kenzi joked. "Even Grant is in the pool."

"I'll pass this time." He leaned down to where Claire was and said, "But send me a copy of the video too. I need that in my arsenal."

"He's joking," Kenzi said then smacked Dax's chest. "You're so bad."

Dax shrugged and his smile widened. "Hey, I love your family, but it doesn't hurt to collect a little insurance now and then."

It was Claire's turn to shake her head. *Note to self: seriously edit the version Dax gets.*

Kenzi put a hand on her hip. "They're your family too."

"Not when they are drunk and half naked," Dax joked without missing a beat. "That's when they're all yours."

"Fair enough," Kenzi responded with a smile.

Viviana rushed over. "Dax, Connor saw you over here. Go back in the house before he does something I'll have to apologize for."

In a confident tone, Dax said, "I don't care how big your brother is, if he tries to pick me up . . ."

"Hey, Dax," Connor called from across the pool.

"I'll be in the house," Dax said, making a hasty retreat with a chuckling Kenzi.

Viviana blew a stray hair out of her face. "What am I going to do with my brothers?"

Claire stood up and gave her a hug. "Just love them and be glad you have family. Sure, they're on the wild side, but look at the joy they bring everyone around them. Ian was worried about today as well, but your brothers give the Barringtons permission to be a little silly—and Dax was right—they need that."

Viviana nodded. "My brothers do know how to get a crowd going. Hope that plays out on the big screen. They don't show it, but they had it tough growing up without our mom, and they're not as confident as they appear. They never had anyone to teach them which fork to use or how to speak in public. I feel so much better knowing you'll be there with them in New York. Grant will make sure they're not taken advantage of, but with you there I also know they won't become a joke. A little success is just what they need."

"I'll do my best," Claire promised.

"That's all we can do," Viviana answered. "Oh, no. Here comes Dale. I hope he's not upset with us."

Dale stood at the edge of pool, hands on his hips. The volleyball came to a quick halt, but resumed after he smiled and asked, "Who's winning?"

We all are, Claire thought. *Today was a win for all of us.*

Chapter Fifteen

THE NEXT MORNING, Ian woke to a pounding headache and way more light streaming through a window than was humane. The warmth at his side confirmed he was not alone. Through barely open eyes, he asked, "Where are we?"

In what felt like a yell, Claire answered, "At The Middle. We flew back to New York last night while you were still shit-faced. Sophie agreed that no one would want to gather today, so we're flying back next weekend. How do you feel?"

"Why are you talking so loud? And so fast?"

Claire chuckled. "Oh, poor baby. Did you really think you could drink Dylan or Connor under the table? Or Kade? They were probably in diapers when they had their first beer."

"Shh," Ian said, feeling around Claire's face until he found her mouth to silence her with a finger over it. After a few minutes of quiet, he said, "Okay, now what were you saying?"

In a softer tone, she answered, "Are you hungry? Tell me if you're going to be sick. I put a bowl on the floor near your side of the bed."

He rolled over to face her. "I didn't drink *that* much."

Claire reached behind her for her phone and held it up so he could watch a video. Although he remembered jumping in the pool, there was a distinct difference in how gracefully he thought he'd done it and how ridiculous he looked in her recording. He reached for the phone.

She let him take it. "Don't bother to delete it, it's already uploaded to my cloud."

He groaned, dropped the phone onto the bed, and reached for her. With her tucked to his side, he closed his eyes again and said, "Just so we understand each other—I could have your cloud wiped as well as all online traces that you ever existed. Piss me off enough, I could wipe you from all government databases as well."

She pried one of his eyes open. "Are you serious?"

Why am I bragging? I must still be a little drunk.

He opened his eyes and decided to play dumb. "What? I'm sorry, I'm fading in and out."

She raised herself onto one elbow, an act that brought his attention to the fact that she was wearing a nightgown. Beautiful as it was, he preferred her naked. It was a conversation, though, for another time . . . one when he could demonstrate why. Right then, the room was doing a little spin and he was a little less certain he wouldn't use that bowl beside the bed.

"Ian . . ."

Shit. I know that tone.

"Yes?"

"What do you actually do for a living? If anyone in your

family knows, they deny they do. And you never talk about it."

He was not prepared to have that conversation—not in the condition he was in. "I don't technically work. I guess you could say I've made some good investments."

"But you have an office."

"Yes."

"And employees."

"That's all true."

"Are you with the CIA?"

He ran his hand lightly through her hair. "If I were, I wouldn't be able to tell you."

"So that could be a yes."

"Or it could be a no."

She cuddled closer to him. He thought she might fall back asleep, but then she asked, "Have you ever killed anyone?"

He could have lied to her, but that had never been part of their relationship. It wasn't a random question. She was too smart for that. She was looking for answers. He'd give her the ones that wouldn't put her in danger. "I have, but never anyone the world isn't a better place without. I intend to leave that lifestyle behind, though."

"I don't understand."

"There is a reason that throughout history the reward for being an accomplished veteran soldier was a promise of land."

"You're a soldier?"

Ian rubbed a hand over his face. "No. Andrew is the hero

of our family, I'm just unsuccessfully trying to make an analogy for the changes I intend to make."

"What kind of changes?"

It was a topic that should have waited until he was less nauseous. There was more he could tell her, should tell her if they remained on their current trajectory. None of it felt like it should be delved into that morning.

Her hand clenched on his chest. "You don't want to tell me."

"It's complicated."

"Complicated as in illegal?"

"Not in a prosecutable sense." When she held his gaze in a silent standoff, he added, "Let's just say the US government is more grateful to me than it is annoyed by me. They won't like it when I tell them I'm done taking their calls, but no one fights on the front lines forever. I have powerful friends and dangerous enemies. If you choose to stay with me, I'll work to lessen the impact of both—but it's not something that will go away."

She searched his face. "If I choose to stay with you . . ."

He groaned and kissed her forehead. "I'm being honest."

"I love that about you." A small smile curled her mouth. "I'm not looking for a man who says what he thinks I want to hear. I don't need reality prettied up. Tell me, these changes you say you're making . . . are they for me?"

It was a loaded question. "Yes and no. I'm ready to—"

"Settle down?" she asked in such a serious tone, he knew he needed to lighten the mood.

He chuckled. "Yes. I see my brothers and sisters with

partners, happier than I've ever known them, and it has made me feel like—"

She kissed him then.

Shut him right up and wiped away his ability to remember what they were talking about with the heat of her kiss and the way she writhed against him. Sure, he wasn't feeling his best, but nature had a funny way of making a man not care about that when the woman he loves kissed him like that.

Loves.

I love this woman.

Right there, head spinning, hands trying to get her nightgown off her, he came to a realization that shook him to the core. *This is it. She's the one.*

He broke off their kiss and looked down at her for a long moment. "Claire, I—"

She stemmed his announcement with another kiss. Was she not ready to hear what he was ready to say? He would have asked her, but when her hands encircled his cock, he told himself there would be plenty of time to talk later.

LATER, AS IAN slept, Claire slid out from beneath his arm, quietly dressed, and headed back to her apartment. She was a jumble of emotions.

Beneath the cleansing warm spray of her shower, Claire admitted to herself that it was panic that had sent her running out of The Middle. She might have imagined it, but he'd looked like he was about to tell her he loved her.

Considering how fast she was falling for him, that should

have been a good thing. Right?

I should have let him say it.

I should have said it back.

Isn't that how love works?

I'm such a fucking coward.

After turning off the water, she stepped into a thick, white robe and padded over to her closet. She hadn't taken a lot, but she had a box of photos she took with her everywhere. She had it stuffed in the bottom corner of her closet because, she told herself, the contents were not important.

But they were.

She took the box to her bed, sat down, and spread the contents out before her. There were photos of her with her mother when they were both young. She remembered feeling loved back then, even though as an adult she knew the situation hadn't been healthy. Back then she thought every family was like hers. She didn't know that some children didn't worry where their next meal would come from. Or knew which bed they'd sleep in each night. She thought all children helped their drunk mother into bed and woke up alone in a house when she didn't come home.

Claire had spent so much of her life hating and missing the woman who was hugging her in those photos. *Love sucks.*

The next photos were of her at her grandmother's house. They said if you look through a person's photo albums, everything you need to know was right there in the pictures. How people stand together or apart. Who chose to stand with whom. Claire had photos of herself and she had photos of her grandmother, but she didn't have any of the two of them together.

Because she didn't want me.

Love really fucking eats ass.

Claire put a photo of her mother next to one of her grandmother. *We should have been a family.*

She picked up a photo of her grandmother. *You shouldn't have the power to hurt me anymore.* Then a photo of her mother. *I wanted you to come back for me. I'm probably lucky you never did, but when I get to heaven the two of us are stepping outside those pearly gates so I can chew your ass out.*

Then I'll hug you.

Because I do love you.

I've always loved you.

Her grandmother stared up at her from the faded photo. *You too. I wish I didn't care about either of you. This would be easier if I didn't.*

Claire fanned her face with both photos. *He loves me.*

I feel like I love him.

What the hell do I know about love?

What if I'm no better at it than either of you?

She tossed the photos into the box and lay back on her bed. Her phone rang. Ian. She didn't pick up.

He texted: **You there? Everything okay?**

She didn't answer him because she wasn't okay, but she didn't want him to see her in the state she was in.

What if this is what my mother felt every time she chose a man over me?

What if I'm destined to follow in her footsteps?

As soon as she heard her inner voice say that, she gave

herself a mental shake. She told her clients that half of their problems stemmed from what they said to themselves in their heads. She believed that.

It didn't mean that she didn't stumble, but she knew better than to let that voice go unchecked.

My destiny is my choice.

I do know how to love.

I love Annie.

I love Kade.

I love Sophie and Dale.

She grabbed her phone but didn't immediately dial. Even though she and Annie were close,· Claire hadn't ever called her for help. *Because I'm afraid to need her.*

I only love people in a small, careful way.

That way they can't disappoint me.

What kind of love is that?

She called up Annie's contact info but took another moment to think. *If after all Annie and I have shared . . . if I can't believe she loves me like I love her—I'll never be able to believe Ian or any other man could love me.*

I'm a good friend.

There's no reason for me to believe she doesn't care.

Claire swallowed hard and faced her fear.

She might not be able to talk now. She's an adult with a busy life. This technically isn't an emergency. Whatever she says—I'll be okay. We'll be okay.

Completely unaware of Claire's mood, Annie answered in a happy tone. "Claire! I was hoping you'd call. I need to hear what Ian said when you showed him the video from yesterday. You did show him, right?"

Claire let out an audible, shaky breath.

In a rushed voice, Annie asked, "What's wrong?"

Just be honest. Unafraid. Myself. Be everything you tell others to be. "Nothing and everything. Annie, I need you. I'm falling apart."

"Oh, my God. Okay. Are you in New York?"

"Yes. At my apartment."

"What do you need?"

Breathe. Be brave enough to ask for what you need. "I think Ian's about to tell me he loves me, and I'm not handling it well. I should be over the moon happy, but I'm thinking myself into dark circles, looking at old photographs, questioning if I'm a complete fraud who has been telling other people how to live their lives when I'm such a mess on the inside. Just that kind of stuff."

"Do you want company tonight?"

"I would love some." Claire's heart burst with grateful love for her friend.

"Send me your new address and I'll find the nearest helipad to your place."

"Thank you, Annie."

"You're welcome. I'm going to hang up for about ten minutes to make arrangements. Then I'll call you back, and we can talk while I head down to you. Does your building have a gym?"

"It does."

"Then when I get there we'll hit the treadmills. You always feel better after a workout."

It was true. Annie knew her so well.

Claire felt bad about ever questioning her friendship. She also felt guilty about having Annie go to all that trouble for something that was only a problem in her head. "You don't have to come down, Annie. You and Kade just got back to Boston."

"Stop right there, Claire. I'm flying down so you'd better make up your couch for me. If you feel weird at all about asking me to come, turn this around. If I said I needed you—as I have so many, many times—would you come to me?"

She'd already proven that. "Yes."

"Friendship goes both ways, Claire. I'm here for you. I love you."

Claire tried not to, but she started to cry quietly. She cried because she felt so blessed to have such a good friend. She cried because she was facing old demons, but she'd just realized she didn't need to face them alone. And Ian? *He might really love me.*

And I might actually be capable of loving him back.

"I love you too, Annie. You have no idea how much this means to me."

"Me too, Claire. Sisters need to stick together."

"Yes, we do." She wiped the tears off her cheeks. "Go, make the arrangements you need to. I'm okay now."

"I—already—did," Annie said slowly. "I did it by text while you were crying. Is that wrong?"

Claire laughed, feeling lighter as she did. "No, it was a productive use of the time."

"I also packed my bag, so I'm out the door. Already kissed Kade goodbye. I'm all yours until tomorrow afternoon. Later if you need me to stay longer. Now, start from the beginning and tell me everything."

Chapter Sixteen

IAN WAS FEELING almost human again. He'd showered, dressed, and downed a few ibuprofen. He would have been in a good mood if he hadn't woken alone.

If Claire had answered his call.

Or his text. Hours had passed, and he had yet to hear from her.

They hadn't argued.

As he'd dressed, he'd gone over every conversation they'd had and was still stumped. Had he missed something? She hadn't said she had an appointment. She'd never left without saying goodbye before.

She might have tried, and I might have been impossible to wake.

She might have lost her phone.

His gut clenched.

She could be hurt.

He considered calling Bradford and having him trace her phone, but he didn't like that side of him to overlap into his private life. No, he'd do this the right way. He'd call her again, go knock on her door. Call Annie if he couldn't find her. Then, if Annie didn't know where she was, he'd track her down just to confirm she was okay.

His phone beeped with a message. Disappointment washed over him when it was from Bradford and not Claire.

Bradford: **Sending an encrypted file.**

Ian: **Regarding?**

Bradford: **The matter you had me looking into.**

Ian froze. He'd been so distracted with Claire and his family that he hadn't contacted Bradford to tell him to call off digging into Pamela's past. There was a chance he was referring to something else . . . something Ian had asked for but forgotten? He typed: **Pamela?**

Bradford: **Yes.**

Fuck.

Not now.

I don't want to find anything anymore. **How bad is it?**

Bradford: **Hard to say, but it supports what your gut told you about her. She's not as innocent as your family wants to believe.**

Ian took the news like a sucker punch. He doubled over and sat on the edge of his couch. **How bad is it?**

Bradford: **Read the file I sent. If you want me to dig deeper, I will.**

Ian's hand tightened around the phone. He needed to think this through. **No, hold off. I'll contact you if I require more.**

Bradford didn't answer because there was nothing left to say. He'd done his job, and as usual he'd done it well. *If I didn't actually want to find something, I shouldn't have sent the best in.*

Tipping his head back, Ian searched for answers on the

ceiling of his apartment. In his hand, waiting for one swipe from him, was something Bradford considered incriminating about Pamela.

A month ago he would have immediately opened the file.

A few weeks ago, he would have hesitated, then done the same.

Now, he was torn.

There was a possibility that the findings weren't as damning as Bradford thought.

Bradford wasn't one to hype things up.

Shit.

He looked down at his phone. *If Pamela was involved in the kidnapping of Kade, and the file contains evidence that she was—how can I not act on that?*

How can I not make her pay for what she did to my family?

He threw his phone across the couch. *As soon as I do, it's game over.*

I lose Kade.

My family.

Claire.

He stood and paced his living room. *Or I delete the file.*

I choose my family and my future over the truth.

I let Pamela get away with a crime, because punishing her isn't possible without punishing the people I love as well.

I don't know if I can do that.

If I delete the file, I'll always look at Pamela and wonder what she did. How guilty is she? What role did she play?

Is the strength my family needs from me one that requires knowing without acting?

That's superhero restraint that I don't fucking have.

I wish I did.

If Pamela is responsible for my mother's breakdown, for all of our childhoods ending too soon . . . for Kenzi having a family she felt she couldn't turn to when someone hurt her . . . I don't know what I'd do.

Who I'd become.

Frustrated on many different levels, Ian retrieved his cell phone and checked his messages. A text from Lance saying he thoroughly approved of Claire.

A text from his father saying he was proud of the men his sons had become.

One from Kade that was short and to the point: **Hope we get together again soon.**

Nothing from Claire.

This should have been a good day—possibly the greatest fucking day of his life. He'd not only patched things up with his family but also realized he was in love for the first time in his life. The real deal.

The choice should be easy.

I should delete the file on Pamela. That would definitely be the easiest route, but he'd never taken the easy path. Frustration simmered into anger—at himself, at the situation, at Bradford for being too fucking good at his job.

To distract himself he turned on the news. The screen filled with a sweaty field reporter describing a situation with pirates seizing a cargo ship off the coast of Somalia. The crew was lined up on the deck, mostly men but a few women. Terrified. Some looked as though they'd been beaten.

Ian swiped to his CIA contact and used encrypted calling. As soon as the call connected, Ian said, "Who is handling the seized cargo ship mess?"

"Kinton is working directly with the president on this one."

"Are they sending in the SEALs?"

"The president wants to use a drone."

"Idiot. Perfect way to get the hostages killed."

"Don't think that hasn't been voiced to him. The ship is in international waters so he is dragging his feet. Off the record, he said since the crew is French this is their problem."

"So he's just going to sit back and watch them die?"

"He okayed a drone strike."

"When?"

There was a pause. "You know I can't give you that information."

"I'm surprised the French Commando Marines aren't all over this."

"Politically, it's happening at a difficult time. Local governments are saying they'll handle the pirate issue on their own. They don't want outside military involvement. We've kept this gem out of the news, but the ship is privately owned. The pirates are demanding a three-million-dollar ransom be paid or they will kill one crew member every four hours starting in the morning. To prove they mean it, they've already executed one. Thankfully, it was before the media arrived."

"How many pirates boarded?"

"Five."

Ian didn't know what to do about the file on Pamela. He wasn't sure how to best handle Claire's retreat, but he was confident he could free those hostages.

His anger needed a release and this was perfect. "Get the media eyes out of the sky, and I'll eliminate the threat."

"Didn't you say you were pulling back? Not taking more missions? Settling down or some shit like that?"

"Do you want those civilians freed or not?"

"Yes. Even if I didn't value their lives, not acting will light a fuse to a political powder keg. We'd rather deny involvement than let the pirates appear to intimidate the United States. The president will of course be told an alternate version. You get in. Get the civilians out. The media will have their story with video; I don't care if we have to create a CGI tsunami. Your name won't be on this at all."

"That's what I want."

"The usual compensation?" Hey, even heroes need to eat.

"No. Consider this pro bono. I'm not back in the game, just this round. This couldn't have come at a better time. I need to clear my head."

"I feel bad for the pirates. Not bad enough to stop you from doing what you do, just glad you're on our side."

"I'll need to get there fast. What do you have that I can hitch a ride on near New York?"

"Just you?"

"And Bradford."

"The new F-16 Viper has a two-seater training variant. It would take calling in a big favor, but there's a general who agrees the president doesn't have control of this situation. We can't get you all the way to the ship—but we could get you to Lemonnier."

"I'll take it from there."

"Then I'll arrange delivery for two—leaving from Stewart National."

Immediately after ending that call, Ian sent a text to Bradford. **We have a job. Meet me at location 9.**

Bradford: **Regarding the matter I sent you?**

Ian: **No, I'll give you the details when I see you. Bring your party gear.** Bradford would know what that meant.

Bradford: **I can be there in two hours.**

Ian: **I'll be there in one. Get your ass in the air.**

Chapter Seventeen

LATER THAT DAY, in a fleece pajama top with matching bottoms, Claire flopped onto her couch next to Annie. Although she hadn't yet responded to Ian, she already felt a million times better. As soon as Annie had landed they'd gone out for chai tea lattes and a vegan meal. The perks of city living: she could get anything in New York that she could in Melbourne.

A long run through Central Park rather than on treadmills had helped calm her.

Enough time with her best friend finally untangled Claire's feelings and fears. She'd shared them, faced them, and even begun to accept some of them as a part of who she was.

Annie hadn't been surprised by anything Claire had disclosed. *Funny thing about a lifelong friend . . . they know more than you think; they're just kind enough to not tell you they do.*

With Annie's help, Claire saw that her attempts to strictly control everything from her thoughts, her diet, and her relationships were protective measures. And the guilt she felt when things were not in her control? Was it truly guilt, or was it fear?

And if it was fear . . . that was okay.

It's possible to be strong and need help now and then.

It's okay to be scared as long as fear doesn't win.

My advice to others isn't bullshit, but it's just as impossible for me to be perfect as it is for anyone else.

"So, I'm going to text him," Claire said, clutching her phone in her hand. "I'll apologize for leaving like I did . . . and for taking so long to answer."

Annie waved a hand at Claire's night apparel. "And if he wants to see you?"

"I'm staying right here. I wouldn't ditch you like that."

Annie laughed. "I'm just going to be sleeping. Ditch away if you want. I'm a big girl."

"No." Claire cuddled down into one corner of the couch. "I do need to talk to him, but I want to hear more about your honeymoon and what it's like to be Mrs. Kade Thompson Barrington."

Annie's smile was wide. "Okay. Then hurry up and call Ian, because I have so much to tell you."

Claire sent a quick text: **Here now. Sorry I left without saying anything.**

He didn't respond.

There weren't even those teasing dots that meant he might be typing.

Nothing.

She frowned. "Should I call him?"

"I would," Annie answered easily.

Claire let out a breath and made the call. It rang once,

twice, three times . . . then went to voice mail. She closed her eyes and said, "Ian, it's Claire. I'm sure you know that from my voice. And caller ID. Anyway. I didn't mean to blow you off this morning. I had some things I needed to sort out in my head. This probably isn't a topic for voice mail. I mean, I don't even listen to my voice messages half the time. As soon as I see that someone called I just text or call them. So, maybe you should do that. Anyway. Call me." She ended the call, laid her head on the back of the couch and groaned. "Why do I sound like a fifteen-year-old?"

Annie touched her arm. "Because you're in love with him, and love makes all of us a little goofy."

Claire opened her eyes and arched an eyebrow. "Did you just call me goofy?"

With a chuckle, Annie mimicked her voice, "I'm leaving you a message that you probably won't listen to because I wouldn't, but if you do even though I wouldn't you should call me."

Thwap. Claire smacked Annie with a pillow.

Annie only laughed more. "So, while we wait for him to call back, what do you want to hear about?"

"Everything," Claire said. She wanted to hear it all. It was impossible to feel sorry for herself while Annie gushed about how good things were with Kade. For as long as Claire could remember, Annie had loved Kade. Seeing them finally together was like watching the most romantic ending of her favorite movie. It gave Claire a warm, fuzzy feeling and hope that she may one day have the same.

PART OF THE reason Ian could do what others couldn't was because he wasn't held back by policies or politics. Unchecked wealth and influence was as close to having a superpower as a person could get in reality.

In short, enough money could tip the scales of any situation to his favor. He and Bradford had made it around the planet in half the time it took most people. They were equipped with heat-sensing rifles, bulletproof vests, and head gear, as well as a few other gadgets Bradford said were still in the prototype phase.

Bradford and his damn fascination with being cutting edge. If he ever wanted a traditional job, which was unlikely since he certainly didn't require the money, Bradford would excel as a weapons field tester for the government. He never said which of his "friends" designed the technology he brought with him, and Ian didn't waste his breath asking. He and Bradford had an unspoken agreement to remain on a need-to-know basis with each other.

They'd both drop what they were doing when the other called. Both were combat trained, but their skills differed after that. Ian was the negotiator, the smooth-talking fixer. If a pretty face and perfect smile were required, Ian went in first.

If the fight started in the alley, Bradford took the lead. Bradford was rougher around the edges. No trust fund in his background. He was brilliant, ruthless, and street-smart. Without speaking he could intimidate most men. He joked that it was due to his tattoos. There'd be no benefit to telling him the truth, it was his scars people saw first. Like a battle-scarred pit bull, growling wasn't necessary. He was a man who *would* shoot if you pissed him off, and if you took his gun, he could still kill you. All it took was looking into his eyes to know not to fuck with him, and that was an advantage that often proved useful. The extensive tattoos on his arms and back were just decorations on an undeniable badass.

They'd met in their early twenties when they'd both had more bravado than brains. Forty young girls had been stolen straight out of a school in a Third World country. Forty. The news had said no one knew where they'd gone. That had been unacceptable to Ian. He'd gone in hot with an enthusiastic but inexperienced team. Bradford had been moved by the same story and had gone to look into how true the details were. Ian had lost half his team. Bradford had gotten stabbed. But they'd found those girls and freed them. What they'd done never made the news. No wars were started over it. Ian made sure of it. The ring leaders of the mass kidnapping were simply never heard from again. Anyone involved who remained understood death would be their sentence as well if the incident was repeated. Bradford ensured that.

Such experiences create tight bonds. Different as they were, Ian and Bradford realized they were strong on their own, but together they were fucking unstoppable.

Playing to their strengths, Ian had arranged for news helicopters to return to the cargo ship, but without filming crews. The pirates wanted to be seen, they wanted their kills to be broadcast. The media wanted the story. Both would get what they deserved rather than what they were expecting. In Ian's opinion, even if the ship's owner came up with the ransom, it was likely the crew would not survive.

Under the cover of the other copters, he and Bradford flew to the far end of the cargo ship. They stood near the open door and exchanged a look. They'd have one chance to fast rappel down without getting shot out of the air. One of the helicopters on the other side of the ship let out a blast of music via a huge speaker: "Hit Me with Your Best Shot." It was enough to make the man on point at the back of the cargo ship turn to see what was happening.

That was what Bradford and Ian were waiting for. They shot down the rope, head first, rifle forward, at breakneck speed, spinning just before they hit the deck so they'd land on their feet.

Bradford immediately threw a disc near the man who was spinning to confront them. There was a bright flash, then the man crumpled to the deck. According to Bradford, the man's communication device would also be knocked out.

"Is he dead?" Ian asked as he kicked the man's machine gun off the side of the ship.

Bradford turned the man over onto his back with his foot. "No. Zip-tie him, but I'll put this on him as well." He clipped another disc to the man's shirt. "It'll zap him unconscious again if he moves."

"Nice," Ian said as he secured the man's arms and legs. In the old days the butt of the rifle would have been as effective, but Bradford liked to show off.

First threat neutralized, Bradford nodded toward the

front of the ship.

Ian raised his rifle and checked the small split-screen monitor on its barrel. Okay, so this technology he liked. On one side he could see heat signatures of anyone, even behind walls. The other side was live feed of the hostages from a circling helicopter. There were two armed men guarding them. Along with two bodies lying in pools of blood about a hundred feet from them.

Two innocent casualties too many, and the pirates were threatening to shoot another hostage before the end of the hour. That life, whoever it belonged to, was the line in the sand. *This stops here.*

Ian was confident as he and Bradford moved through the ship. This was what they did. This was where his instincts never betrayed him.

A man reached out from behind one of the lifeboats and made a grab for Ian's rifle. Ian blocked the move, grabbed the man's arm, pulled him forward using his own weight against him, and sent him to the ground, disarming him before he hit the ground. The man rolled and scrambled to his feet.

"You speak English?" Ian demanded with his rifle pointed at the man's head. "If so you have one chance. Surrender now and you live."

The man reached down and pulled a knife out of a belt. He snarled something, raised the knife and was about to throw it when he was taken out by Bradford.

The man had made his choice and every shot Bradford made was a kill shot. He wasn't what some would call a man of mercy, but killers didn't deserve mercy—not in Ian's book.

They exchanged a nod and moved forward through the ship.

As they went, Ian swept the area with infrared for any more surprises. Nothing. They moved forward. On the way over, they'd studied the layout of the ship and planned their sniper spots.

It had to go perfectly or more innocents would die. Ian took a high position. Bradford went low and on the other side. Two bullets. Two synchronized kills and they could go home.

Silent fingers went up. Three. Two. One.

The drop of the two armed pirates to the deck was followed by the sound of several of the crew screaming then cheering. They frantically looked around while hugging and moving away from the carnage. Ian and Bradford stayed out of sight.

It was time to pull out.

A door beside Ian flew open. A woman bolted out and leaned over the railing beside Ian. Tears were streaming down her face. She called out to one of the fallen men then turned to Ian.

For just a flash, Ian didn't see her face, he saw Claire's. He saw his death in her eyes and didn't feel expendable anymore. He wanted a life with Claire, wanted that family he'd imagined with her and those children he could almost picture.

Whatever she thought was wrong between them, he'd

make it right.

I love her.

I should have said it.

He saw the woman before him reach for her weapon, but she didn't shoot. She looked scared, and he wondered if she'd joined the pirates willingly. Where food and resources were scarce, women had even less options than men. She was someone's daughter. Possibly someone's mother. Could they save her as well?

She fired her gun.

Missed.

But a hot pain shot through Ian's left butt cheek, and he fell forward from the force of it, toppling over the railing and down to the deck below. Funny how something could happen so fast and still slow down enough to give a person time to think. Ian's last thought before he hit the deck below was of Claire and all the things he should have said to her.

Then everything went black.

CLAIRE WAS SITTING in her office two days later. It didn't help her concentration that Ian's office was a few doors down, and she still hadn't heard from him. From Ian's secretary to the man across the hall who wouldn't tell Claire what his job description was, everyone claimed they didn't know where Ian was.

How could they not?

Claire had distracted herself by going with Dylan and Connor to meet with the casting director for their first movie. Connor was scripted as a country doctor. Dylan was a city bad boy. Claire located an acting coach for both and helped them settle into their New York apartment.

Grant and Viviana brought her father to the city to see where Dylan and Connor were staying. He was a large man, but not nearly as large nor as loud as either of his sons.

If it weren't for Ian, Claire would say things were working perfectly. The production company had already referred a couple actors to her. She was interviewing each carefully. This time she wanted quality, not quantity. The money would come, but she wanted to fill her time with meaningful interactions.

Still staring out the window of her office, Claire answered her phone.

"How are you doing today?" Annie asked. She'd reluctantly left the day before.

"I'm okay. I spoke to a couple of potential new clients." Although Claire was grateful that she'd come, she was also okay on her own. One thing Claire was good at was pushing forward, regardless of what she was going through.

"That's good. So, nothing yet from Ian?"

"Nothing. I don't get it. I understand that he might have been miffed that I didn't answer his text, but I didn't take him for a sulker. And maybe I read the situation wrong, but I really felt like we had a connection." She stood and rubbed a hand over her eyes. "I don't know."

"No one here has heard from him either."

"Do you think something happened to him?"

"I asked that, and Asher said Ian disappears on a regular basis, sometimes for weeks at a time."

"Where does he go?"

"Asher wouldn't say."

"You don't think that's weird?"

"You try to find a normal Barrington."

Touché.

"So, that's it? What am I supposed to do with that?"

"There's nothing you can do. Wait, I guess. Ask him all your questions when he surfaces."

"I don't know if I can wait it out. Would Sophie or Dale know where he is?"

Annie made an awkward sound. "Claire, don't ask Sophie about this. You don't want to be the person who asks her where one of her children is when she finally has all of them back. I can't imagine that going well."

"You're right. I just want to do something. In the movies, I'd break into his apartment and look for clues. Imagine."

"Ian would lose his mind. He doesn't come across as someone who appreciates the dramatic."

"Maybe. I have a feeling Ian has a whole other side to him."

"Like what kind of side?"

"I don't know, and it scares me that I don't. Is he a criminal? Does he have another family in a foreign country? For all I know he's part of an act in a traveling circus. I really have no idea. So what does that say about our relationship?"

Annie sighed. "I wish I knew."

"Me too. I've never felt so close to a man, but I know that doesn't guarantee he feels the same. Maybe he wasn't about to say he loves me. Maybe the look I saw in his eyes was goodbye, and I only saw what I wanted to."

"Stop. You don't know how he feels, and you won't until he comes back."

"Want to hack his computer with me?"

"No."

"Tap his phone?"

"No. And you don't really want to, either. Waiting for answers is hard; if he's the man you think he is, he'll be worth the wait."

Annie would think that. She waited for Kade most of her life. Claire couldn't see herself doing that. "I'm giving him one week, Annie. One week."

"And then what?"

Claire sat back down at her desk and slumped forward. "I don't know."

Chapter Eighteen

IAN WOKE IN an all-white room. He expected to be in pain, but everything was still delightfully fuzzy. He vaguely remembered okaying a surgery after the private island hospital had discovered a bullet fragment lodged deep in the muscle of his left buttock. Considering recent studies were linking fragments left in to lead poisoning later for patients, his doctors were vigilant.

And he was blissfully extra high on morphine.

"You're awake," Bradford said as he entered the room.

"I am. I'm also officially renaming you Sherlock . . . Holmes, that is," Ian said with a laugh. He couldn't explain why, but the comparison felt hilarious.

"Still drugged up, I see. I'd ask you how you feel, but I doubt it's much."

"For short, I'll call you Sherlie. Sherlie Holmes."

Bradford took a seat beside Ian's bed. "So, what will your story be about the cast? Looks like you'll have it for six weeks."

"What cast?" He looked down at his arms. "Holy shit. When did I get that?"

Bradford nodded toward Ian's IV. "I'll have what you're having."

"I totally forgot I broke my arm."

"Do you remember getting shot?"

"Vaguely. I remember the fall clearly though. It happened in slow motion." He remembered how scared the woman who'd shot him had looked. "Is she dead?"

"No. I didn't know why you held your shot, so I neutralized her and she's now in the hands of the Somalian police." Bradford propped his feet up on the edge of Ian's bed. "This was sloppy, Ian. I don't mind dying for something important, but I'm not following you anywhere else if your head isn't on right."

Ian would have said the same had the situation been reversed. "I love her, Bradford, but everything is such a fucking mess."

"The woman on the boat?"

"No. Claire."

"The Australian woman you keep asking me for more information about even though she's as squeaky clean as they come. The worst I could find on her was sometimes she stashes potato chips in her desk and then secretly disposes of the bags. Like it's a crime. Lady, you're beautiful. You're allowed to have a damn chip now and then."

Ian's eyes rounded. "You investigated her that thoroughly?"

"Hey, best way to judge a person's character is to observe who they are when they think they're alone."

"You scare me a little."

"Good."

Ian laughed. "I used to be scary. Now—it's like I've lost my touch."

Bradford laughed. "What the fuck are you talking about?"

Ian sighed and told Bradford all about how Connor and Dylan had kidnapped him at the wedding. To give Bradford credit, he at least tried to keep a straight face. "Connor thinks it's funny to pick me up and hug me like I'm a child. I can't hit him; he's Viviana's brother."

"Oh, poor baby. You'll be okay, Ian."

Despite Bradford's sarcasm, Ian continued, "Sure, laugh it off. You're not the one who has to play nice with Tweedle Dee and Tweedle Dumber. I'd love to shake them up, just once. But I'm already the asshole of my family. That title used to be Asher's, but I'm the one everyone is worried about. At least I was, until I told them they shouldn't be, but I spoke too soon. There is a very good chance I'm going to destroy my family."

"I don't think you're plotting to slaughter them, so I'm going to stop you there. I'm not a therapist. I don't have family. I don't want family. In my experience, you're better off without them, so I'm not the person you should talk this out with." Bradford lowered his feet to the floor and was about to stand.

"Bradford. I need to ask you something important."

Bradford settled back in the seat. "What?"

"Morphine is like a truth serum. Am I a spy?"

"No, you're not."

"Thank God, because my head is really fuzzy right now, and I don't want to give away government secrets, but I can't stop talking. Don't let me tell the nurses anything important."

"Do I have permission to smother you with a pillow if you look about to?"

"No." Bradford was kidding.

I'm pretty sure he's kidding.

"Fine. Then I'm not going anywhere because you do know too much—about both of us."

Ian felt a surge of euphoria that was unrelated to the situation. He'd never experimented with drugs and didn't like not feeling in control of his emotions. There he was trying to have a serious conversation and part of him was close to giggling. Giggling. He tried to raise his left hand to his face but only succeeded in knocking himself in the head with his cast. "Ouch."

"Easy, there, Ian."

"Is my face messed up too?"

"Yeah. It's bad."

"Fucking fantastic."

"Oh, wait. You've always looked like that. Sorry."

"Asshole." Ian shook his head, but the move made him dizzy. "I'm done, Bradford."

"Done with the hospital? They're not done with you yet."

"No, I'm done with pirates, rebels, dodging bullets. I'm ready for a job that doesn't want to kill me. One with a little plaque with my name on it. I want my staff to be able to say what I do. I don't want to kill anyone anymore. That's what I saw in that woman's eyes. She didn't want to be there either. I want a family, Bradford—with Claire. If I'm dead I can't have children with her."

Bradford sat back, folded his arms across his chest, and said, "That's pretty much how death works."

Ian moved to sit up then winced. "Why does my ass hurt?"

"Bullet."

"Oh, yeah." Ian moved his left arm up and down like a wing. "And this."

"Lord give me patience. Or enough drugs to knock him back out."

"I never thought I'd want children. Children are just little parasites who grow up to be big ones." Ian lay back down. "I don't care. I want my own parasites. In a house. With a dog. And a yard. I'll wear the kid on my back, take him to the zoo, be one of those dads."

"I can't see you ever doing that."

"I never thought I could see my brothers with children, but they're having them and they look so fucking happy. I want to be happy. I think I could change a diaper. I mean, I once held a man's intestines in place for the medics while they worked on his partner and that was disgusting but I did it. A diaper can't be worse than that."

"I have no idea."

"How hard could being a father be? When you're little . . ." Ian laughed. "No, when they're little. You shouldn't raise a baby when you're a baby."

"Oh, boy."

"I wouldn't care if it's a boy or a girl. I could teach my son martial arts. I could scare the shit out of any boys who ever came close to my daughter."

"If you taught your daughter martial arts, she could scare the shit out of them herself."

"You're a fucking genius." Ian sighed. "I can't marry Claire."

"You don't have to tell me why."

"And it's your fault."

"I'm sure it is."

"You sent me that damn file about Pamela. I had just told my family they had nothing to worry about from me. I was done looking for something on her. Then you sent me that damn file. I'm not a saint. How am I not going to read it? And if she was involved in kidnapping Kade, I'll want to kill her. I won't, but I'll want to."

Bradford nodded slowly. "Now I get it. You brought all that shit with you to Somalia."

"Yep."

"Idiot. You could have gotten us both killed. Is that what you were hoping for?"

"No. I want to live. I just—" He stopped to think, which wasn't easy. "I just wanted to do something that made sense. I don't know what to do about Pamela or Claire or my family. On the boat, with those hostages, I knew. The right path was clear."

Bradford ran a hand through his hair. "You're a better person than I am. I'd be traveling your path but without the guilt. If she kidnapped Kade, she shouldn't get away with it."

Ian almost threw up in his mouth. "Is that what you found? Did she take him? Was it all a lie?"

"Nothing that clear cut. We should probably talk about this later when your head is clear."

"Tell me," Ian said hoarsely.

Bradford didn't answer at first, then he said, "I tracked down her old physician in Aruba."

Ian whistled. "You are good."

"A month before your brother disappeared, Pamela had a miscarriage. Opportunity? She worked at the same clinic the baby was taken from. She claims she didn't know who the parents were, but I'd argue it wasn't that large of a clinic and your parents were big-name patients. Means? Her brother. Motive. I'm not a doctor, but losing a baby probably does something to a woman's head. Your instincts are usually spot-on. I'd bet my life that the reason you think she's guilty is because she feels guilty. And why would she if she's innocent? The dots are all there, it's only a matter of connecting them."

A wave of relief washed through Ian. Bradford didn't have solid evidence. "Don't. Don't connect them. I don't want to know." He stared at the ceiling then met Bradford's gaze again. "Fuck. Keep digging. I need the truth. But then what? I lose everything. I hurt everyone I care about. Either way I'm fucked."

Bradford neither agreed nor disagreed.

Ian closed his eyes for a moment. His head was so foggy he was struggling to remember what he was upset about. "I love Claire. We have this place we call The Middle. I bought it for her, but she wanted her own place. I don't want to change her. She doesn't want to change me. So we meet in the middle. She wants a partner. So strong. So fucking perfect. I want to grow old with her, but maybe my love isn't the good kind. Maybe she was right to leave while I slept."

"You are pathetic on morphine."

"This is how I really feel. She deserves to be happy. I want her with a man who will treat her well, give her that family. I want to be that man, but maybe I'm not him. Can you love someone and still be the wrong choice for them?"

Bradford pressed the call button for the nurse.

"Yes?" the nurse asked from a speaker on Ian's bed.

"Is it possible to give Mr. Barrington something to help him sleep?"

"Is he uncomfortable?"

"Sure," Bradford said.

"I'll be right there."

"I'm not in pain." Ian flapped his broken arm.

The nurse rushed into the room. "What seems to be the problem?"

Bradford answered, "He's not comfortable with how morphine makes him feel. He'd rather sleep off the worst of it and have the pain rather than be a pain."

The nurse cocked her head to one side at the end of Bradford's comment. "I'm sorry, he'd rather be in pain?"

Ian rolled his head to the side. "I would?"

Bradford nodded. "Trust me on this one."

A few hours later, Ian woke up alone to a throbbing pain

in both his arm and his ass. Clearheaded, he remembered everything that led up to his fall over the railing, but not much after that. He remembered Bradford coming to see him, but he couldn't remember what they'd talked about.

He called for the nurse. She informed him that Bradford had arranged for him to be moved over to a suite on the other side of the hospital where he could rehab with privacy. There would be medical staff on call, but he could heal in luxury.

Ian reached for his phone. Bradford had left him a message: **Running an errand. Be back in a few days.**

Beneath that were several messages from Claire. She was worried about him, but he wasn't ready to talk to her. He sure as hell wasn't going to tell her where he was, so what did that leave for him to say?

Nothing.

He tossed his phone down.

"How long will I have this one?" Ian lifted his cast.

"Six weeks," she said. "You could fly with the cast, but your friend said you'd rather stay here until you're healed. Is that what you want to do?"

"I don't know."

Her smile was gentle. "That's normal after an injury. Give yourself a few days and you'll be right back to feeling like your old self."

Ian laid back and groaned.

Right back to his normal self?

He didn't know what that was anymore.

Chapter Nineteen

CLAIRE STEPPED OUT of the elevator on the floor of her apartment. She was tired, but happy with how her day had gone. Dylan and Connor had practiced their scripts with their acting coach then asked her to come to day one of filming. She smiled as she remembered how well they'd done. The camera loved them. Connor came across as a big, softhearted hunk of a hero. His character was a doctor and medical terms rolled off his tongue with savant-like smoothness. Dylan was playing a street-savvy, military brat. Rough around the edges. Dangerous. He pulled it off well. So well, that Claire wouldn't be surprised if the next role someone offered him was in an action movie.

Lost in her thoughts, she didn't notice the man standing beside her door until she was almost upon him. The hair on the back of her neck rose. He was not only a large man, as tall as Ian, but built like a tank. Square neck. Bulging muscles covered by tattoos and several scars. The way he watched her made her nervous. "May I help you?"

"Claire Wendell. I have a car downstairs to take us to a private airport. From there we'll fly to an island off the coast of Singapore so pack accordingly."

"I'm sorry," she said, taking a cautious step back. "Who did you say you were?"

"I didn't. I'm a friend of Ian's, and I'm here to take you to him."

She remembered something Ian had said about having powerful enemies as well as friends. "If Ian wants to see me, he knows my number."

"He's not in a position to call you right now."

That sent a shiver through her. She took another step back. "I don't know what that means, but I can assure you I'm not going anywhere with someone I don't know. I've seen a lot of movies where that ends badly." She took out her phone. "I don't want to call 911 but I will if you don't leave."

The corner of his mouth twitched with a half smile. "They'd never get here in time."

She gasped. She believed him.

His expression softened. "What would it take to convince you to go with me? Short of calling Ian."

She backed farther away. "Does his family know you?"

"No."

"Okay, then really this isn't going to go well." She took out a small Mace sprayer.

"Mace? Really? That might stop a dog. And never let someone know you have it before you try to use it." He sighed. "Listen, I'm not here to hurt you. I'm trying to help. Call the police, but know that this is why I don't normally get involved in personal shit. When I spoke to Ian he went on and on and on about you. I felt bad for the guy, but I'm not going to force you into a car. If you want to see him, patch things up, have your little family of parasites, with the house and dog, then this is your chance. If not, I tried." He waited a moment, then turned to walk away.

"Wait." *This is crazy. Dangerously crazy.* "If you really do know Ian and he did talk about me, tell me something only he and I would know."

The man turned slowly and Claire backed up again.

He was leaving. Why the hell didn't I let him?

Some of his dangerous vibe faded as he scratched the back of his head while thinking. "He said a lot of shit and not all of it made sense."

That didn't sound good.

Then the man added, "If he could meet you in the middle, he would. But this time you have to come to him."

The Middle. Only Annie knew about what she and Ian called the apartment Ian had bought for her. Ian wasn't someone who would share information like that with just anyone. "What's your name?"

"Bradford."

"Ian has mentioned you."

That did not appear to make Bradford happy. "He did?"

"He told me you were someone I could trust if I ever got in trouble. He gave me your number." She held up her phone as if the number would be there on her darkened screen.

"Then go pack because I've already given too much time to this."

Claire touched his arm. "Is Ian okay?"

"He will be. He'll heal."

"Oh, my God. What happened?"

Bradford turned and looked down at his watch. "Do you know what we'll have on our flight? A lot of time for you to ask me that again and for me to tell you it's better if you hear it from him. He's not in danger now, but he does need your help. I'm not going to stand here all day. You have ten minutes to pack. Come if you want. Don't if you don't."

"Where is he?"

"I'll be down in a black car in front of the building. You now have nine minutes." With that, he left.

Claire packed faster than she ever had in her life. Still, she cursed the slowness of the elevator and Mrs. Pottstone when the elevator stopped and opened for her. She was in her late seventies, still very independent, but loved to talk. "Haven't seen that handsome man of yours around lately. If it's over, I have a grandson your age who would adore you just for your accent."

"I'm sure he's wonderful," Claire said while pressing the close button as soon as the other woman was inside the elevator.

Looking down at her luggage, Mrs. Pottstone said, "Going away for the weekend?"

"Yes," Claire answered evasively.

"Anywhere interesting?"

"No, not really."

A knowing smile spread across Mrs. Pottstone's face. "Oh, I remember those weekends. My son wants me to move into an assisted living building. I hear they are a hotbed for sex. At my age, do I really want multiple partners? I already have Mr. Franklin from 4B, and he knows how to fix my cable when it goes offline."

Oh, boy. Claire hit the lobby button again even though the elevator was already descending to it. "I think you should do whatever makes you happy."

"Are you happy? When you first moved in you were glowing. I had that same look when I met my first husband. I'm still mad at him for dying. He was my one big love, you know? I've had other men in my life, even married one of them, but Wilton took my heart with him when he went to heaven."

The elevator stopped at the lobby and opened. Claire wanted to rush away, but what Mrs. Pottstone had said struck home. She had to know. She bent to pick up her luggage and asked, "Would you do it all over, even knowing you'd lose him? Or was losing him so hard you wish you'd kept your heart to yourself?"

Mrs. Pottstone stepped out of the elevator with her then smiled. "I would marry and lose Wilton a thousand times if that's what it took to have one more day with him. Nothing is forever. If you're given a chance at that kind of happiness, you grab hold of it, and you savor the shit out of it. Love is always worth it."

Claire put her bag down and gave Mrs. Pottstone a hug, before saying she really needed to go.

TWELVE MINUTES.

Shit.

Would he still be there?

Flustered and sweaty, half expecting to see him driving off, Claire burst out of the front door of her apartment building. Bradford was still there, leaning against the side of a car. He made a show of checking his watch. "You're late."

"You're still here," she said, trying to catch her breath. "I didn't think you would be."

He took her bag and tossed it in the trunk. "I knew you were coming, and I really am a nice guy."

She slid into the passenger seat, surprised he held the car door open for her. She waited until he was behind the wheel then asked, "Then why the ten-minute limit?"

He shrugged, "That's how long it takes me to pack."

Claire's nervous energy bubbled out as a laugh. "Seriously?"

"Seriously." She might have imagined it, but she could have sworn she saw a twinkle of humor in his eyes.

In some ways it was difficult to imagine a friendship between this rough man and Ian, but in others it wasn't. Ian was more than his smooth exterior. "How long have you known Ian?"

"Nearly a decade."

"And his family doesn't know you?"

He glanced at her. "I'm not the kind of friend people bring home to meet their parents."

They drove along in silence for several minutes, then Claire added, "You should be. Sophie would love you. Warning though, she has mother hen instincts. Once she feeds you, she starts to think of you as one of her own. I found it disconcerting at first, but it's real." Claire swallowed as emotion clogged her throat. "She'd like you."

Without looking away from the road, he said, "I don't have a family anymore, and I am better off for it."

"I used to say that—then I met the Barringtons. I didn't have the storybook family growing up."

"I know. I wrote the reports on you."

"Oh, so you're the one who scared off all my clients?"

"Did I? I might have come on too strong with a few of them, but I have a low tolerance for bullshit." He was quiet a moment then added, "Sorry. I lectured Ian on being distracted, but I haven't been myself lately, either. I was irritated with Ian for calling in a favor for something any local PI could do, but I shouldn't have let it affect your business."

It was not only an apology, but a sincere sounding one at that. "Thank you. It's okay, though. It all worked out for the best. Having to start over freed me to come to the States and explore other opportunities here."

"That's an optimistic spin on a shitty situation. I know your job is to spew stuff like that, but I don't buy it. If our roles were reversed, you'd be dead."

Claire's hand clenched her seat-belt strap. *Okay, then. Remember not to cross Bradford.* "I'm not spinning it. Bad things happen, but I don't allow negative thoughts to remain in my head."

"Denial. I've heard it works for some. I prefer a more realistic approach to life."

They pulled onto a small private road that wound its way

to a long runway where a private jet was waiting for them. Bradford parked, unloaded two bags from the trunk of the car, then spoke to the pilot briefly while Claire followed behind and told herself this was all perfectly normal and safe.

If Mrs. Pottstone would go through the pain of losing her husband a thousand times just to have another day with him, I can do this.

A few minutes later, seated in the jet, Claire looked across at Bradford. He had a laptop open and was typing away even as the jet took off. "Bradford?"

He paused his typing but didn't look up. "What?"

"Ian is lucky to have a friend like you. Thank you for coming to get me."

He shot her a side glance. "You shouldn't trust people as easily as you do. Sure, I knew about The Middle, but I could have hacked into your smart TV and simply overheard you and Ian discussing it."

Claire sat up straighter, then trusted her gut and said, "You didn't do that."

"No, I didn't, but I could have."

"Why do you want me to be afraid?"

"Because the world is a fucked-up, dangerous place. I don't want to spend the rest of my life rescuing you from every asshole you go off with who says he knows Ian."

Claire relaxed into her seat. The more Bradford spoke the more she could see how similar he was to Ian in some ways. They both talked tough, but beneath that, they were loyal. In medieval times they would have been knights . . . riding off to save damsels in distress. The idea brought a smile to her lips. "I'll be more careful in the future, Bradford."

"Good," he said gruffly and put earbuds in.

There was so much she wanted to ask him. How had Ian gotten hurt? How injured was he? Where exactly were they going?

A steward offered Claire a glass of champagne. She accepted it, hoping one or two of them might help her sleep to pass the time. Bradford didn't look like he wanted to talk but with about a fifteen-hour flight, she was confident she'd wear him down and get some information out of him before they landed.

She glanced at Bradford again. It saddened her to think he didn't consider himself worthy of being taken home to meet Ian's parents. Did Ian realize his friend felt that way? Claire doubted it.

Once the dust settled, that was something Claire wanted to change. Sophie had such a soft heart. She would dote on Bradford.

Kade wouldn't trust him at first.

Asher would challenge him in some way.

Grant would offer to help him protect his financial assets.

Lance would design a beautiful home for him.

Kenzi would make him laugh.

And Dale—he'd probably give him a hug, because like Sophie, he had a huge heart.

Good things can come out of bad times. The Barringtons are closer and stronger now because of what they went through. I hope the same ends up true for Bradford. He's scarred on the inside as well as the outside.

Bradford turned and took out one earbud. "Do you need something?"

It was an opening anyway. "I used to think family had to be a blood relation and I didn't win in that lottery. But I'm changing my definition, and it's making everything else okay. Nothing can change what I didn't have growing up, but I can change who I become because of it. I said yes to going with you, because I believe in love, and I finally see I'm worthy of it. Ian makes me happy, and I want to savor the shit out of my time with him. I hope you find that with someone because when you do, you'll see that no matter how fucked up the world is . . . love changes everything."

"You're not going to talk the whole way to Singapore, are you?"

So cold. So abrupt. *He's scared.* "I never had a brother, but if I did, I'd like to think he would have been like you. If this all works out, and Ian and I have that house, those little parasites, and our dog . . . will you promise that you'll join us for the holidays? Don't accept being a fringe friend. You deserve better than that."

"Stop. I'm not one of your clients."

"Oh, you're coming to Christmas and that holiday where Americans overeat and watch football."

"Thanksgiving."

"Yeah, that one. Pass the fucking turkey."

Bradford laughed. "You must drive Ian crazy."

"I do," Claire said with a chuckle. "Now, how did he get

hurt?"

Bradford wagged a finger at her. "You're good."

"I meant everything I said, but we also have about fourteen hours before we land. You can tell me now, or you can tell me later, but I will know what happened before we land."

"Really?"

"Really. Just start with how you met and work your way to how he got hurt."

"Why would I do that?"

"Because we're family?" She shot him a smile.

Bradford rolled his eyes, but he didn't replace his earbud. Instead his expression turned nostalgic and he said, "Ian's been trying to get himself killed since the day I met him, but it's always for a good cause, and I respect that. We were in our early twenties and we'd heard about these young girls who'd been kidnapped right out of their schools. I didn't know Ian back then. We were just two people who saw something so fucked up we couldn't not do something about it. I don't like many people, but Ian didn't have to give a shit about those girls. He's rich. Connected. Most people like that are usually more worried about the next party they'll attend than what happens halfway across the globe to people who have nothing. Ian had some men down and some injured. He wouldn't leave either. We freed those girls and doled out a satisfying amount of justice as we did. We've been friends ever since."

"Do you work for the government?"

"When they need us and we agree with their goal."

"Ian wouldn't tell me what he did."

"Because he cares too much to eliminate you if you talked."

"But you don't?" A shiver went up Claire's back, then she caught a hint of amusement in Bradford's eyes. "You think you're pretty funny, don't you?"

Bradford shrugged. "My investigations are thorough. You're an intelligent woman who hasn't had so much as a parking ticket in the last five years. And you're loyal. I saw what you did for Annie and Kade. Ian needs someone like you on his side, but it's not all pretty. We've made some real enemies over the years. You need to know that before you start thinking life with him would be a fairy tale."

"I don't want the fairy tale," Claire said. "I want a good man who will love me and my children—never consider either a burden. Someone I can be myself with and not worry that I'm too much for him to handle. Enemies don't scare me. Everyone has them. His just have faces and names. I could get killed for my wallet or run over crossing the street. Survival is about being prepared, being careful, but not giving in to the fear."

Bradford nodded. "So, Ian got shot in the ass then fell over a railing and broke his arm."

"Oh, my God. When? How?"

"Pirates. It's a funny story, actually." He paused and rubbed his chin. "Do you want the real details or are you squeamish?"

Claire had to think about that for a moment. "I guess the real ones? I'll tell you if it's too much."

It was an enlightening flight after that. By the time they were making their descent to the private island where Ian was a patient, Claire felt like she'd gone on an emotional roller coaster.

Ian had a whole side to him she was positive no one in his family had the faintest idea about. Some of Bradford's stories were like listening to war movies Claire normally didn't watch because she didn't like to put those images in her head. Ian had lived them.

He was as dangerous and as complicated as she'd fantasized, but this wasn't a fantasy. Could she build a life with man who didn't value his own—even if every cause he'd chosen had been a noble one?

She remembered him saying he'd make changes for her. She wasn't sure she wanted to be the reason he stopped defending those who couldn't defend themselves.

Bradford had told her a lot—more than Ian probably ever would have. *Sophie, you've taught me well in the fine art of a loving interrogation.*

What do I do with what I know?

"I love him, but how could we ever have a normal life?" Claire only realized she'd asked the question aloud when Bradford answered.

"There's no such thing. And if there was, would you even want it?"

Claire let his words sink in. "You're right. There's nothing normal about the Barringtons, and I love all of them. You'll hate Asher when you first meet him, but he's really funny when you get to know him. They call him the hammer because he's over the top sometimes, but he's married to the sweetest woman and when she looks at him, he just melts. You have to love him for that alone. Oh, hold on, I can't wait for you to meet Clay."

"I know who he is."

"Of course you do, but have you met him?"

"No."

"He has more money than God, and loves to tease Asher about having more than him, but he's not the snob you'd think he'd be. He and Andrew have built a veteran rehab center that's fully independent from the government and privately funded. Oh, my God, and Viviana's brothers—"

"The meatheads . . . and I carefully use the term with affection."

"Ian really did tell you everything."

"He was on some powerful painkillers after his surgery. I have a loose idea of how I might help Ian calm them down."

Claire rushed to say, "They're gentle giants. Like two big kids stuck in men's bodies. Don't hurt them."

"Hurt—never. That's Ian's family. Scare the shit out of . . . maybe." He smiled.

Claire shook her head. Part of her wanted to tell him to not do anything, but she'd also seen what Connor and Dylan considered a prank. Sometimes the best medicine for someone was a taste of their own.

She looked out the window of the jet as it lined up with the runway. Everything Bradford had told her about Ian was circling in her head. The stories might have scared another woman off, but the thread that Claire had heard through all of it was that Ian cared.

And when he cared he didn't sit idle and wish things were different.

How could she not fall more in love with him now that she saw how his protective nature wasn't confined to his family? Maybe it wasn't so much that he didn't value his life, but rather he deeply valued the lives of others. It was what made a fireman rush into a burning building when he knew someone was trapped. It was why Annie and Kade trained for search and rescue in Australia's Outback. Claire hoped Ian would one day tell Kade some of the stories Bradford had shared with her. Kade had always stepped up and helped those around him. He and Ian had more in common than they realized.

"What aren't you telling me?" Claire asked as the jet bounced then rolled along the runway. "Ian's not in danger. His injuries aren't life threatening. So, why is he still here? What does he need from me?"

"Now that is something only he can tell you."

Chapter Twenty

UNMEDICATED, IAN STOOD on the balcony of his suite at the hospital's rehab center. If it weren't for the medical staff, his accommodations might have been at any luxury resort. This was where people came when they wanted to recover discreetly.

His surgeon had promised the scarring on his ass would be virtually nonexistent, as if that mattered. From what little he'd seen of the other patients, though, he understood the surgeon's focus on perfection. Face-lifts were the norm. The facility catered to tummy tucks, breast implants as well as reductions, liposuction, and a host of other age-defying procedures Ian had no interest in. He'd asked his surgeon how many bullets he'd removed.

His answer? One. Ian's.

Not shocking.

Nor was it a surprise that Bradford thought such a place was where Ian would want to be treated. Although they understood each other on many levels, sometimes Bradford saw Ian through the lens of how different their childhoods had been. Ian's may not have been ideal, but he'd never known the insecurity of where his next meal would come from. He'd never endured physical or mental abuse.

Bradford had.

They'd saved each other's asses countless times over the years. Funny that someone who had never met Ian's siblings could feel so much like a brother to him. Bradford had always said he didn't want to meet them and Ian had accepted that on face value. Lately, though, Ian was beginning to look at the people in his life with fresh eyes.

Bradford had no one.

He said he didn't want a family.

In some ways he reminded Ian of Claire. Bradford would cringe at the comparison, but it was neither a compliment nor an insult. They'd both had difficult childhoods—both survived but had difficulty trusting relationships.

Ian winced as he bent to lean on the railing, and the move pulled at the stitches on his buttock. He looked down at the cast on his arm and sighed. Five more weeks.

This will be fun to explain.

He could easily make up a story about how it had happened, but he'd never lied to Claire.

Claire.

He'd almost called her so many times. Every day that he didn't was a weight on his heart. He wanted to be with her. She wasn't the problem. He was.

He was stuck in an ugly cycle of self-loathing and indecision. The old him would have already opened the file Bradford has sent. He'd already have passed judgement and doled out justice and not have given a second thought to what anyone thought of his actions.

He didn't want to be that man any longer. He was afraid, though, that he still was—would always be nothing more than that man.

Not opening the file, though, was slowly bringing him to his knees.

Rather than sleep, he lay in bed each night asking himself how he'd ever live with himself if Pamela turned on Kade one day . . . turned on anyone in his family . . . and the signs that she would were in the file he refused to open. *The right path used to be so clear to me.*

"Miss me?" a female voice said from behind him.

Ian straightened and spun on his heel. "Claire." He strode toward her, reached out to sweep her up into his arms but stopped when his left arm rose awkwardly due to the cast. Seeing her again gutted him in a way that was both amazing and unsettling. God, he loved her. There were things he was confused about, but what he felt for her was achingly clear. "How did you—Bradford."

"Yes." She closed the distance between them then caressed one of his cheeks while saying, "I'm not happy with you."

"Then we have something in common," he answered as he inhaled her scent. "I should have called you."

She dropped her hand to her hip. "Yes, you should have. Especially after you were shot."

"Shot," he repeated the word. How much had Bradford told her? *How much should I tell her?*

The answer came to him while looking down into her

eyes. *She deserves to know everything.* "I've never lied to you . . ." he started.

She cut in, "That's the only reason I'm here."

They shared a long look. This was part of why he loved her. She was a force to be reckoned with and wouldn't settle for less than his best. At an early age, he'd taken on the role of problem solver for his family. Claire didn't need someone to save her.

She's here to save me.

He blinked back an emotional response to that realization. With Claire, not only could he have that family he'd recently discovered he wanted but also the kind of equal partner he'd never imagined he'd find.

It's time to let her see the whole me. "You once asked me if I work for the CIA. I do and I don't. Over the years, I've become someone they call in when situations are too complicated for traditional responses."

"I know. Bradford told me all about it on our flight over." She searched his face. "I don't approve of violence, but I understand that sometimes it's the only way to resolve a situation. It was a long flight, and I cringed my way through a lot of 'war stories,' but I've also had time to process them."

That didn't sound like Bradford at all. "He isn't normally so free with information."

A soft smile stretched her lips. "He knows I love you."

Whoosh. Ian rocked back on his heels, then cast and all, he pulled her into his arms and murmured, "I love you too, Claire," before he kissed her with all the passion and longing he'd been holding back. It was a kiss that left them both shaken, breathing heavily, and staring into each other's eyes.

"Then don't fucking get yourself killed," Claire said in a husky voice.

A chuckle rumbled out of him before he said, "I thought I had all the answers. I was a cocky bastard before we found Kade. I don't know what the fuck I'm doing lately. If you'd met me before—"

"We wouldn't be together. I'm not looking for perfection. I'm all kinds of fucked up in my head. I like you more because you're real and you make mistakes. Help me through mine and I'll help you through yours."

"I didn't swear as much before I met you," he joked.

"Fuck. Fuck. Fuck," she said with a smile.

He hugged her closer. "If you insist. It might be a little painful with my stitches, but I'll do my best."

She laughed then laid her hands flat on his chest and her expression turned serious. "Why are you here, Ian?"

"My family would have too many questions about my injuries."

She shook her head. "Okay, maybe that's part of it, but we both know there is more going on here. I understand why you might not want to tell me. I'm like that too. I'll share when things are going well, because it's easy to. When things fall apart, when I feel lost, I hide it. Is that what you're doing here? Hiding?"

He wanted to deny it. He took a deep breath. He'd been raised to keep his feelings to himself, but hers was an opinion he valued, and they'd always been real with each other. "Bradford found something on Pamela."

She shuddered against him. "What?"

"What he found is in a file on my phone. Just sitting there, waiting for me to open it."

"I'm so sorry."

It wasn't the reaction he expected. He thought she would mirror his own harsh assessment of his indecisiveness. "I should just fucking open it. I don't know what my problem is."

She raised a hand to his cheek. "I do. You love your family. You want to protect them—even from yourself. You're a good man, Ian. Being a cocky bastard is easy. Being a good son? A good brother? Kind when cruel would feel good? That's the hard stuff."

He buried his face in her hair. He could live with that version of himself. "I almost deleted it, but there might be something there I need to know . . . a hint of a threat to come. What if it's not something I can live with? What if she's taken other children?"

"When did you find out about the file?"

"The last morning we were together—after you left."

Her eyes filled with sadness. "I shouldn't have done that. I'm sorry. I've worked with a lot of couples who love each other but didn't have what it took to make it. Love is a feeling, but it's also a decision—a promise. It's sticking it out through the good and the bad. I was afraid. I know what it's like to be left behind. I won't leave you again, but you have to promise me the same thing. If you want me to be all in with you—you need to be all in with me."

Her strength humbled him. People joked about their

spouses being their better half, but he saw the truth behind the humor. He'd pulled away when he should have pulled her closer. He saw that now. "I'm all in, Claire. I was wrong. I shouldn't have pulled away."

She sniffed. "No, you shouldn't have. But you know how you could make it up to me?"

He smiled. "Sex so wild it pops my stitches?"

She laughed and covered her eyes. "Easy there." She stepped back. "I was referring to the file. I think we should open it—together."

Together was the word that wiped the last of his reservations about opening it away. "Yes." He took her hand, led her to the couch, and took out his phone before gingerly sitting down beside her. He didn't feel out of control as he located the file. She was his safe port in the storm, and she'd given him a fresh view of even himself. He loved his family. His indecision wasn't a weakness. His biggest mistake was thinking he had to solve this alone.

He didn't. He had a partner.

He bent down and gave her a brief, deep kiss. "I won't let you down again."

"I'm sure we'll both make mistakes, but—"

"Shut up and kiss me," he growled.

She smiled and did. It would have been easy to let their passion take them further, but the things he was imagining doing with her required a little more mobility than he was currently capable of.

He broke off the kiss and simply held her to his chest for several long moments. When their breathing returned to normal he picked up his phone again and opened the file, holding the phone so they could read it at the same time.

Hazy memories returned to Ian as he read. "Bradford told me some of this while I was on morphine. I can't believe I forgot it. I've always felt that there was something off about Pamela. He thinks she feels guilty because she is guilty."

Claire let out a shaky breath. "He makes a solid argument against her. She must have been devastated when she miscarried her own child. Maybe she wasn't in her right mind."

"Maybe." The rage Ian expected to feel didn't come. He no longer wanted Bradford to be the one seeking the answers. "There's only one way to know for sure."

"You're going to ask her."

"No," he said as he cuddled Claire to him. "*We* are."

She smiled up at him, and a spark of passion lit her eyes. "How much pain are you in?"

His face warmed. "Nothing I can't deal with."

They had to get a little creative, and not every position they tried worked out, but when one didn't, they laughed, adapted and overcame. Later, sated, his stitches still intact, he lay on the bed with his unbroken arm wrapped around her. "Just how much did Bradford tell you?"

She raised her head. "Enough for me to know I don't want you to stop what you do for me. The world needs people like you."

"It's not exactly a lifestyle that lends itself to having a family—and I want that with you."

She seemed to think that over, then smiled. "If you trust

me, I have an idea for a way we could meet in The Middle."

A WEEK LATER, Claire stood with Ian outside the door of Pamela and Dave's hotel suite in Boston. Ian had called ahead and told her there was something he needed to discuss with her. She'd agreed to see him more readily than either had expected her to.

"Do you think she'll be alone?" Claire asked.

"Hard to say," Ian answered.

"If Dave is with her, don't let that change how blunt you are. You have questions. You have a right to ask them." As she heard herself, she cringed. It was hard sometimes to turn off the coaching side.

Ian smiled indulgently and gave her hand a gentle squeeze. "We've got this."

We. Her heart warmed.

Pamela's husband, Dave, opened the door. "I knew this day would come. All I ask is that you hear her out."

That wasn't promising.

Ian agreed, and they stepped inside. Dave closed the door behind him.

"Does Kade know we're here?" Claire asked.

Dave shook his head. "He wouldn't have handled it well, but I understand why you have questions. I didn't in the beginning, but Pamela has opened up to me about everything that happened back then." He pocketed his hands and took a moment before saying, "I'll get her now."

Claire looked up at Ian. "He looks—defeated. What do you think he knows?"

Ian's jaw tightened, and he closed his eyes for a moment. "Whatever it is, if it doesn't put my family in future danger, I'm prepared to accept it—for Kade."

Overcome with emotion, Claire hugged Ian so tightly he protested with a laugh. "Hey, save your enthusiasm for later, Tiger."

Tears blurred her vision as she leaned up to kiss him. "You're a good man, Ian Barrington."

He smiled even as he kissed her back. "I'm trying."

"Ian. Claire," Pamela said in a tight voice as she entered the room. "Why don't we have a seat?"

Claire and Ian settled onto a couch. Pamela took a chair close to them. Dave stood behind her.

"Thank you for seeing us," Ian said smoothly.

She nodded and clasped her hands on her lap. In the silence that followed, tears filled her eyes.

Claire leaned forward. "We're only here with questions, Pamela."

The older woman dabbed at the corner of her eyes. Her husband put a hand on her shoulder. "You found out about my miscarriage, didn't you?"

"We did," Ian said.

"And that makes you question whether I saved Kade or stole him." It wasn't a question. Pamela was simply stating what they all knew. "From the first time I met you, Ian, you looked at me like I was guilty of something."

Ian cleared his throat. "Are you?"

A tear escaped and ran down Pamela's cheek. She brushed it away. "I don't know. Maybe. I was in my second trimester. His name was Mathew. Or it would have been. He never took his own breath of air. I was a nurse. I've asked myself a thousand times if there were signs I missed. He was alive inside me. Kicking. Growing. Then he wasn't. He simply wasn't. I delivered him at the hospital, but it was a stillborn delivery. He was already gone."

Claire gripped Ian's hand tightly. "Oh, my God. I'm so sorry, Pamela."

"They already know that part, Pam," Dave prompted gently.

Pamela sniffed and nodded. "Right. I was out of my mind with grief. I'd wanted that baby badly. I'd left Dave for a man who'd turned out to be nasty when his niceness wore off. He couldn't have run away faster when he found out I was pregnant, but I hadn't cared. I would have my baby. Finally someone of my own—someone who wouldn't leave me. Then I lost him, too."

Claire understood that feeling all too well. Her heart went out to the woman.

Pamela continued, "Then my brother brought me this healthy baby boy. Everything I said about how that happened was true. I had no idea my brother would take him. I was scared when my brother didn't come back and everyone started dying."

In a calm, measured tone, Ian asked, "Did you know who Kade was?"

Claire held her breath and prayed. *Please don't let her have known. Please don't give us a reason to hate her. Ian said he's prepared to accept it, but forgive her? I don't know if I could if she knew.*

Pamela shook her head. "I'd heard the Barringtons had lost a child, but didn't make the connection. Kade was premature, but not enough that he needed medical care. What I didn't do, though, was ask questions. I took Kade and ran to Australia. Did I have to run? Could I have found out what had happened if I'd gone to the police? I don't know. Maybe I didn't want to know. I told myself I didn't ask questions because I didn't want someone to come after Kade, but what if that wasn't the only reason? What if I kept quiet because I didn't want to give him back? What does that say about me?" She began to sob into her hands.

Claire moved to kneel next to her. Her heart was breaking for everyone involved.

Ian stood and walked over to where Pamela sat. He looked down at her for a moment before saying, "They would have killed him. Had you asked questions back then, neither you nor Kade would be here today."

Pamela continued to cry. "You don't know that."

He came to a stop beside Claire. "I do. Everyone who knew anything is dead. Except Helene's uncle, and he was kept alive only to cover the tracks. No one was safe while my aunt was alive. She would have never let you live."

Dave let out an audible breath. "I told her the same, but she doesn't believe it. The guilt you sensed when you met her was the shame she's carried with her all this time."

Pamela nodded and raised her eyes. "I've tried to be the best mother I could be, but I never went looking for his birth mother—not even when he was old enough to hear the truth. I kept him from you. I kept all of you from him, and I hate myself for it."

Ian met Claire's gaze briefly and thought she saw emotion glistening in his eyes as well. The pain on all sides was so real, so deep. When he spoke his voice was deep with emotion. "You have nothing to feel guilty about, Pamela. You saved my brother. And you gave him a good life. He'd argue it was a great one. I know meeting with me wasn't easy, but what I learned today brings me peace. Let what I've told you bring the same to you."

Fresh tears poured down Pamela's cheeks. "I've lived with the guilt for so long."

Ian bent to look her in the eye. "I'm well acquainted with guilt. I saw in you what I felt in my own heart. I'm coming to the sobering realization, however, that none of us are invincible. We're all just doing our best to figure out this crazy ride we're on."

Dave interjected, "I agree with that one hundred percent."

In a shaky voice, Pamela said, "I suppose I'll have to tell Kade."

"I wouldn't," Claire said, rising to her feet and tucking herself under Ian's arm. "Some things don't need to be said."

"Is that so?" Ian asked with an arched eyebrow.

"Unless it's me, and then I should always be in the know," Claire added.

"Glad you clarified that." Ian smiled.

Dave stepped forward and held his hand out to shake Ian's. "What happened to your arm?"

"Boating accident," Ian said with a straight face then winked at Claire.

"Ian can be so clumsy," she concurred.

He smiled in challenge, but didn't correct her.

Life with Ian would never be boring, but she wasn't looking for boring. She'd found a strong man who would stand by her side, let her take the lead now and then, and had a heart of gold beneath his tough exterior. Not everyone would see that side of him and she was okay with that. She saw it.

Dave saw it.

Bradford did as well. He hadn't even blinked when she'd asked him to help Ian land an oversight position in the top-secret foreign relations department of the CIA. When the offer had come to Ian, Claire had tried, but failed, to look surprised.

It hadn't taken much persuading to pry her involvement out of her. He wasn't upset, though. In fact, he accepted the offer after negotiating for Bradford to run the department with him. Instead of fighting on the front line, they'd make sure those who did had the accurate intel and the highest of high-tech weapons.

She wished she could have called Annie and celebrated each step she took forward with Ian, but there'd been too much she had to figure out on her own first. Plus she couldn't have kept their visit with Pamela a secret from Annie—and Ian had just proven that Claire's trust in him had been deserved. Love was a leap of faith a person had to take on their own sometimes.

Pamela stood and hugged Claire then Ian. "Thank you. I didn't expect the kindness you've shown me today."

Cast and all, Ian hugged her back as if this had been a simple visit with friends that was concluding. "It's time we all move on. We have too much to celebrate to live in the past."

After the hug, a smile spread across Pamela's face, and she glanced down at Claire's left hand. "Do the two of you have news to announce?"

Claire froze. She loved Ian. He loved her. They were moving forward together. But the whole drop-down-on-one-knee proposal? She hadn't let herself think that far ahead.

Ian tucked Claire against his side. "Not yet."

Claire was relieved and disappointed, a confusing mixture of emotions. Her breath caught in her throat. "It's still so new."

Ian dipped his head and whispered in her ear, "Breathe, Claire."

She did, one deep, calming breath, then she said, "I'm fine."

His expression turned tender. "It's okay to not be. I'm a wreck every time you look at me."

She smiled then. "As long as I'm not alone."

A slow smile spread across his face. "Alone is one thing you are not." It was so easy to imagine all the places that smile would take them.

A happy sigh escaped Pamela, reminding them that they weren't alone. Claire blushed when Ian announced, "We should get going."

It felt so obvious when she added, "We don't want to be late for . . ." She stopped when she couldn't think of an excuse fast enough.

Ian shook Dave's hand, then ushered Claire toward the door. "An important appointment."

"A very important one," Claire agreed, then blushed more when she saw the knowing expressions on Pamela and Dave's faces.

Dave chuckled and walked toward the suite's door to open it for them. "Run along, you two. Life's too short to miss *appointments*."

Claire and Ian were laughing as they entered the elevator. She wrapped her arms around him and rested her cheek on his chest. "Ian?"

"Yes?" he asked between kisses.

"Thank you."

"For what?" He raised his head.

"For letting me in."

With his good arm, he hugged her to his chest. "I have a lot more than that to thank you for."

She cocked her head to one side. "Don't hold back."

He smiled gently and tucked a curl of her hair behind one of her ears. "Will you ever let me have the last word?"

"Probably not," she joked with a widening smile. "I have a lot to say."

"I'm okay with that." He laughed and pulled her against him, his lips hovering over hers. "As long as it's never goodbye."

Feeling playful as well as turned-on, she writhed against

him and promised, “Never goodbye.”

They spent the rest of the night at The Middle exploring creative ways to thank each other, until they lay on the couch sated and spent in each other’s arms.

She traced a design on his bare chest. “Annie told me Clay is planning a pool party. Your whole family is going.”

“Are they?” Ian asked without opening his eyes.

“Have you seen any of them since we’ve been back?”

“No.”

“The party sounds like fun. Would you like to go together?”

He rolled over so they were face-to-face. “You’d go without me?” His expression gave none of his feelings on that possibility away.

She propped herself up on one elbow. “In a heartbeat. I love your family.”

His mouth stretched with a warm smile. “And I love that you’re as independent as I am.”

She smiled back. “I’m glad you do, because I’m probably not going to change. And I don’t want you to. Every story Bradford shared brought home how much I don’t want to hold you back. I’d rather we be independent together.”

“Independent together—I like that.” His eyes shone with love. “We should raise our children the same way.”

“Our children?” Had she heard him correctly?

“Sure. All seven to ten of them.”

“Seven to ten?” The room tilted then righted. She slapped his chest playfully. “You’ve lost your mind.”

“Okay, how many do you want?”

Her mind was spinning. “I don’t know. I haven’t thought that far ahead. We’re still figuring this out.”

“Are we? Marry me, Claire. When I’m with you I’m the man I should have always been. I don’t have to figure anything else out to know that I want to spend the rest of my life with you.”

Her first answer was a deep kiss delivered with such enthusiasm she forgot to watch out for his broken arm when she rolled him over onto his back. When he groaned, a little with pleasure and a little with pain, she raised her head. “Sorry.”

“Don’t be,” he said in a deep, pleased voice. “I’m taking that as a yes.”

She rained kisses on his lips and face. “Bet your sweet ass it’s a yes.”

“Looks like you and I are going ring shopping.”

A giddy feeling washed over Claire, but she tried to temper it with facts. “We shouldn’t. Diamonds are symbolic of love now only because of an ad campaign in the early 1900s. It’s all a romanticized public relations-based tradition, but . . .”

He silenced her with a kiss. “Claire, I’m going to buy you a ridiculously large diamond and propose again when my family is present.”

When the kiss ended, she sat up. Although she wanted to believe that things could work out for her like that, more realistic expectations were safer. She sought the right way to explain to him that he didn’t have to propose again. Love for him welled within her and spilled out as tears as she faced her fears as well. "Of course I want that, but don't feel that you have to—"

"Have to?" He frowned. "Claire, you can believe in me. I'm not ever going to leave you."

She swallowed hard and met his gaze. "I love you. I'm just scared, I guess."

He kissed her temple and held her closer. "Last year, if you'd asked me what scared me I would have said nothing. I didn't worry about things or second-guess myself. Grant found Kade and my life turned upside down. Then I met you and started to want more than I had. I'm ready to settle down, Claire, and I want to be with you. It's absolutely terrifying to imagine myself as a father, but then I look at you, and I see a lifetime of laughter, a house full of love, and two kids or ten kids I really don't care. I now understand how my father gave up his career for my mother. It would be an easy choice for me. You're what matters, Claire. If you want to take it slower, you say so."

She buried her hands in his hair as his words calmed her fears. "Ten kids? Are you crazy?"

"I am crazy," he said with a smile. "For you. Can you handle it?"

"I believe I can." She traced a hand down the strong muscles of his neck, across his solid pecs, then encircled his cock that was proudly readying for another round. Would it always be as good as it was that day? She'd always warned her clients that it couldn't be.

But maybe she'd been wrong.

Sophie and Dale, Pamela and Dave, Hazel and Mitch

had all been married a very long time and still looked at each other with love.

Being with someone was definitely a whole lot scarier than being alone, but she wanted that family Ian had described . . . that house full of love . . . a lifetime of laughter, and she wanted it with him. *Not sure about the ten kids, but I do love the idea of a big family.*

She would have told him all that, but she decided to do something else with her mouth. After all, the poor guy had a broken arm, and she'd read articles about the healing power of orgasms.

Chapter Twenty-One

CLAY LANDON COULD afford the best, and no one had ever accused him of being subtle. It didn't surprise Ian that he had rented a mansion with a veritable indoor water park. Who even knew there was such a thing in New England—Clay apparently. A long lazy river was housed in a glass enclosure off to the side of a home that could only be described as an estate.

Claire whistled as they entered the pool area. "Wow, this is . . ."

"A lot," Ian agreed. Dressed to swim, his family was scattered around the pool area. "That's Clay for you. He likes over the top. Dax said he's hoping to recreate the night we all got drunk and played volleyball at my parents'. FOMO—for him it's a serious condition."

Claire glanced around. "Not looking that wild today."

Asher was dipping his laughing son into the lazy river then lifting him above his head only to dip him again, all while a smiling Emily looked on from the edge. Lance was beside him with Willa and their twins in swim floats.

Not wild at all.

Comfortable.

Right.

Kade called out Ian's name. Ian tensed as he turned slowly in the direction of his voice. Claire's hand closed around his.

Hand in hand with Annie, Kade stopped just in front of them. His closed expression made his mood difficult to determine. "You went to see my mother."

"We did." It had once annoyed Ian to hear Kade refer to Pamela as his mother, but it didn't that day. She'd raised him in a loving home, sacrificed for him, worried for him, and was still in his corner regardless of what it might cost her. What was that if not a mother?

"She called us," Annie said. There was a hint of disappointment in her voice. "I'm surprised you didn't say anything about going to see her."

Claire's hand tightened on Ian's. "I should have. It was a busy week. My phone didn't ring with a call from you either."

A silence followed that neither he nor Kade interrupted.

It was a standoff the likes of which only best friends could have. Annie blinked first. "I shouldn't have made you feel like you had to choose a side."

Claire blinked back tears that were filling her eyes. "I should have trusted that either way we'd still be solid, because in my heart we always will be."

"Mine too," Annie said, stepping forward.

Dropping Ian's hand, Claire met Annie halfway and the two hugged.

On the other side of them, Kade rubbed a hand across his forehead. "I wish you'd told me you were going to see her, but she told me what you said and how much comfort it brought her."

Ian nodded. "Right or wrong, I had to know the truth. I feel that I do now. In the family department, you won the lottery. You have two sets of incredible parents. When I look at Pamela and Dave, that's all I see now."

Kade let out an audible breath of relief then turned his attention to Claire. "I said my share of things I regret. Claire, I'm sorry you got caught in the middle of all this. You've been nothing but good to Annie and me. You deserved better."

"This has been a wild ride for all of us." Claire hugged him as well. "Honestly, I'm too happy to spend another moment thinking about everything we all could have done better. I love both of you, I love your whole family, and I'm head over heels in love with your grumpy brother."

"Hey," Ian protested with a chuckle. "Who are you calling grumpy?"

"Is intense better?" Claire asked with an overly innocent expression as she returned to his side.

He arched an eyebrow.

Claire, Kade, and Annie burst out laughing.

After a moment, he found himself smiling as well. "I prefer *intimidating*."

Hugging an arm around his waist, Claire said, "How long do you think it'll take Kade to realize his brother is a big marshmallow beneath all that growl?"

"Hush, woman, before you ruin my reputation," Ian countered with a chuckle.

He looked up to find Kade smiling in approval. Then he nodded toward the other side of the pool area. "Your friend Bradford is here. In a suit. Did you tell him it's a pool party?"

Ian's mood sobered as he scanned the room for his friend. He was talking to his mother, who was in a flowing cover-up. "I told him."

Claire said, "He looks so uncomfortable."

Kade added, "I tried to talk to him, but it went about as well as our first conversation."

Ian nodded. "I wasn't sure he'd even come. Let's go save him from my mother."

Sophie smiled as she spotted all of them approaching. "I hope you brought your bathing suits."

"Of course." Ian leaned down to give his mother's cheek a kiss. "Hello, Mother."

Claire gave her a kiss and hug next. "Where's Dale?"

"Babysitting," Sophie said lightly.

"Lance's twins?" Claire asked.

Without missing a beat, Sophie said, "Viviana's brothers." She turned to Bradford. "Have you met them?"

"I have not had the pleasure, but I've heard all about them," he said.

Ian's eyebrows shot up. *What did I tell him about them?*

"I hear they like a good prank," Bradford added. "I'm looking forward to meeting them."

Ian choked on a laugh and exchanged a look with Claire.

We should call him off.

She smiled and replied with a surprisingly unconcerned shrug.

Really? She's the nicer half of us so if she's okay with it . . . prank on, Bradford.

"It's good to see you here, Bradford," Claire said. "Sophie, did you know they've been friends for nearly a decade?"

Sophie searched Bradford's face. "Is that so?"

Ian clapped a hand on his friend's shoulder and said, "Sure is. I've lost track of how many times he's saved my hide."

Sophie stepped closer to Bradford and said, "Thank you for looking after my son."

"You're welcome." Bradford didn't meet her eyes, but her comment seemed to please him.

Claire piped in, "Which hotel are you staying at, Bradford?"

He didn't say.

"Hotel?" Sophie exclaimed. "Bradford, you can't stay at a hotel."

Oh, Claire was good.

Bradford didn't look like he knew what to say. Ian could have rescued him, but decided his parents might be exactly what Bradford needed.

Sophie continued, "Bring your things over tomorrow morning. Dale and I would love the company. Our house used to be overflowing with children. Now it's just us."

He shook his head and opened his mouth with what looked like a refusal, but the arrival of Grant, Viviana and their young son, Sean, robbed him of the opportunity.

Balancing the baby on his hip, Grant held out his hand to shake Bradford's. "Nice to finally meet you. Heard you and Ian will be working together—in a capacity we can finally talk about."

Ian shot his brother a warning look. *Not in front of Mom.*

Bradford shook his hand then Viviana's. "Looks that way."

Sean reached out a hand toward Bradford, but Bradford ignored it in a way that made Ian wonder what had happened to his family. He refused to discuss it.

Seemingly unaware of the moment of tension, Grant smiled at Claire. "And you?"

Claire wiggled her eyebrows and leaned closer to stage whisper. "Things are going well."

Viviana clapped her hands together. "I knew it."

"How well? Like proposal well?" Sophie asked. She greeted her young grandson with a smile and a kiss before turning her attention back to Ian. "If you're about to do what I think you are, we should get Dale. He can't miss it."

"I am and he won't," Ian assured her.

"Oh, my God, is this really happening?" Viviana exclaimed and started calling to everyone to gather around.

"It is now." Ian laughed and hugged Claire.

Claire's grin was huge. "You did say you wanted to propose in front of everyone."

"I've been known to change my mind when it comes to you." Knowing her as he did, it was hard to believe he'd ever doubted her. He watched his siblings, some still wet from the water, with their spouses, their children, and friends as well gather—and asking her to be his felt right. Dale joined Sophie. Connor and Dylan waved from behind the crowd. He waved back.

"Let's do this." Ian dropped to one knee and opened a box that contained a ring Claire had helped him choose. It was a modest, round diamond in a cathedral setting. Classic but with engraved scrollwork on the sides. Unique like Claire. Strong like their bond.

"Claire Wendell, I knew you were trouble from the first moment I laid eyes on you. Now that you've completely destroyed my desire to remain single, will you marry me?"

She bit her lip as she seemed to need to think it over. "Ian, you are every bit as much trouble as I've ever been. I don't think anyone else could handle either one of us, so yes, I'll marry you."

They were both laughing as he slid the ring on her finger and stood. "Thank God," he said then kissed her to a round of applause from those watching.

The rest of the night flew by in a happy daze. Ian loved every moment of watching his family welcome Claire and the joy it brought her to finally belong.

Ian's whole family, including his sometimes confrontational brothers, had welcomed Bradford. It was as if they realized accepting Bradford was like accepting all of Ian—the side he'd always shared with them as well as the side he'd kept concealed.

Realizing how many times they'd come close to not making it to this place, Ian hugged Claire to him and whispered,

"Thank you."

She smiled over her shoulder at him. "For what?"

He couldn't articulate how deeply she affected him or how grateful he was to have her in his life, so he kissed her and murmured, "Everything."

She snuggled back against him. "The ones you should really thank are Dylan and Connor. When you think about it, they brought us together."

The memory of how was slowly becoming amusing. "That they did. It's probably best that we not say it, however. Wouldn't want to encourage them."

"So true. No telling what they'd get into then." She chuckled then looked around. "Speaking of that, I don't see them. It's not like them to leave a party early."

Ian scanned the room. "I don't see Bradford, either."

"You don't think . . ."

Across town in an abandoned storage building:

CONNOR SUTTON SLOWLY regained consciousness in the darkness of a sack over his head and with the uncomfortable realization that his wrists and ankles were bound. The last thing he remembered was stepping outside with Dylan and Bradford, to help Ian's friend bring in something from his vehicle.

"Dylan?" he asked as he tried to free his hands from their restraints.

"Yeah," his brother answered from beside him.

"Are you also tied up?"

"No, I'm free and fucking playing a video game."

No success, Connor tried his feet. "We may have pushed Ian too far."

"You think?"

"Hey, you know what isn't helping right now? Your negativity. There's a chance this is just a joke."

"My ass is freezing on this damp floor. My head is pounding from whatever drug Bradford used on us. Doesn't feel like a joke."

The sound of a door opening had them both falling silent. The sack was pulled first off Connor's head then Dylan's. Bradford stood there, his suit pushed back on one side so they'd both see the gun holstered beneath it.

When Bradford didn't say anything, Connor decided to break the ice. "Hey, Bradford."

The look he gave them was as cool as any killer's would have been. If it was a prank, Bradford didn't seem amused by it.

Dylan said, "Did Ian ask you to teach us a lesson? If so, consider us taught."

Still Bradford said nothing. He simply stood there.

Creepy as all hell.

Connor cleared his throat. "He knows we were only having some fun when we did this to him. No harm, no foul, right?"

Dylan added, "He should be grateful. All's well that ends well, right?"

Nothing.

After a moment, Bradford growled, "Are you two too stupid to know when to be afraid?"

Connor sat up straighter. "Hey, no need for name calling."

"Shut up, Connor," Dylan muttered.

"No, I won't shut up," Connor said. "Okay, so we chose not to go to college. So what? Dad needed our help. Maybe we don't know as many fancy words as you do or know which fork to use when, but I can change the oil in an excavator's gearbox with my eyes blindfolded. Loose track? Would you know how to deal with foaming of the fluid and erratic actuator movement?" When Bradford held his silence, Connor added, "I didn't think so. You probably don't even know how to inspect the heat exchanger to ensure the core isn't blocked. Dylan was born knowing how to do that. There are all different kinds of intelligent in this world, and just because we're not your kind doesn't mean we're any less smart."

Beside him, Dylan sat up a little. "You really think that, Connor?"

Connor nodded and chucked his shoulder into his brother's. "You know I do. You are gifted when it comes to routing out the cause of internal leakages."

"Stop," Bradford said, raising a hand. "Just stop."

"Thanks, Connor," Dylan added. "That means a lot to me. If we die today, you should know I've always envied how you're better with women than I am. They like you as soon as you smile at them. Me? I have to convince them I'm not an ass first." He nodded toward Bradford. "I bet he has the same problem."

Bradford frowned.

Connor made a sympathetic sound. "That's not true. Women fall all over both of us. My problem is I'm too nice. That's what women tell me. Sure, they like the sex, but then they say I'm not a challenge. I'd kill to have one of them think I'm an ass just once." His eyes flew to Bradford's. "Not kill. Killing is bad and never a good idea."

Bradford blinked once. Blinked twice, then smiled. "What do you say we go for a beer?"

"I'm in," Connor said without hesitation.

Dylan gave Bradford a look, then shrugged. "Okay, me too."

"Get up," Bradford said. Connor's eyes widened when he took out a knife, but all he did was cut the rope around their wrists then handed it to them so they could free their own feet. "Stop fucking hugging Ian. He doesn't like it."

"Is that what this is about?" Connor asked. "Geez, all he had to do was say so."

Dylan freed his feet, stepped away from the rope, and tossed the knife back to Bradford. "He's so sensitive."

Bradford caught the knife with ease, sheathed it, then gave them both a long look and chuckled. "He really is."

THE END

Not ready to say good-bye to these characters? Sign up for my newsletter via my website www.ruthcardello.com/newsletter and stay informed about releases.

Preorder Reluctantly Alpha due out March 4, 2020

Printed in Great Britain
by Amazon

15818632R00169